SURVIVE

SURVIVE

Alex Morel

Survive
First published in Great Britain in 2013
by Electric Monkey, an imprint of Egmont UK Limited
The Yellow Building, 1 Nicholas Road, London W11 4AN

Text copyright © 2013 Alex Morel
The moral rights of the author have been asserted

ISBN 978 1 4052 6413 6

1 3 5 7 9 10 8 6 4 2

www.electricmonkeybooks.co.uk

A CIP catalogue record for this title is available from the British Library

52578/2

Typeset by Avon Dataset Ltd, Bidford on Avon, Warwickshire
Printed and bound in Great Britain by CPI Group

EGMONT

Our story began over a century ago, when seventeen-year-old
Egmont Harald Petersen found a coin in the street. He was on
his way to buy a flyswatter, a small hand-operated printing
machine that he then set up in his tiny apartment.

The coin brought him such good luck that today Egmont has
offices in over 30 countries around the world. And that lucky
coin is still kept at the company's head offices in Denmark.

Fear is something I don't think you experience unless you have a choice. If you have a choice, then you're liable to be afraid. But without a choice, what is there to be afraid of? You just go along, doing what has to be done.

—Margaret Hastings, World War II plane crash survivor
From *Lost in Shangri-La*, by Mitchell Zuckoff

Part I
Prepare for Takeoff

Chapter 5

Part I

Prepare for Takeoff

Chapter 1

It is ten minutes before ten, and normally I'd be staking out a chair for Group. That's the kind of thing you worry about in an institution like Life House. I guess that's good, in a way. The challenge of Group is to find a chair as far away from Old Doctor as possible without sitting too close to Big Stink, otherwise secretly known as BS. BS is Ben, and he's the only boy on Life House D, which is specifically for cutters and suicides, and he smells like urine baked at three-fifty for forty minutes. You don't want to sit next to BS for an hour. I mean he is extra sweet and all and we've had some nice conversations, but an hour of inhaling his fumes can cause brain damage. Sometimes the logistics are tough, so I get there early and wait. I'm a planner.

But today I'm not participating in Group. Instead, I'm

flying home to New Jersey for the first time since arriving in Idaho three hundred and forty-five days ago. My plane leaves in exactly six hours, nine minutes, and thirty seconds according to the pocket watch my father left me. It is old, but I trust it. He's dead, but I still trust him more than anyone else I know, and I certainly trust his pocket watch a lot more than I trust the airlines and the schedules they almost never keep. But I can't worry about that now. The fact remains: I'm leaving Life House, my home away from home for the past year, in six hours and nine minutes flat. Ticktock ticktock.

I'm here at Life House because a year ago I had an "incident." The professionals, otherwise known as my doctors, have labeled it an *attempted suicide*. Me and Old Doctor (he's the chief of chiefs around here and my doctor too) haven't agreed that that is what actually happened. I might have just been cutting or maybe I just wanted attention from my mother. These are two theories we've considered during the last year.

"And until we agree on what happened," he has said many times, "you may call it what you wish."

In two hours, 12 p.m. to be exact, I will board a bus and leave here forever. Over the past six months, I've been accumulating *Progress Points*—speaking in Group, two points; mentoring other girls, three points; sharing and

4

communicating during non-required social activities, five points—all acts of good faith in pursuit of one goal: freedom. The points added up, enough to earn me this week-long trip to celebrate Christmas with my family.

What the doctors don't know is that it's all been a lie: everything I've done, every "hello" to Drs. Crimshaw and Gallus, every perceived act of kindness to my suite mates, Beth and Sam and BS, every faux revelation delivered with a tear or two to Old Doctor has been in service of a secret plan.

Here's what you need to know: When I get on that airplane tonight, I will never arrive home. My body will land in New Jersey, but me, the airy part that lives inside my body, my soul if you must, will not. When the lights go down and all the people nod off for a short nap, I will unfasten my seat belt and quietly walk back to the restroom and take a handful of kryptonite and go to sleep. Forever. And when the plane lands, and everyone is scurrying to find their luggage and looking for signs for ground transportation, I'll be on my own flight to oblivion.

Chapter 2

Deceiving my friends and doctors isn't devious or self-ish; it's just pragmatic and necessary to achieve my goal. I'm a planner, as I've said a few times already, and if I don't know exactly what's ahead of me, I lose my shit. That's probably why I'm here. Life is impossible to plan, so I'm constantly losing my shit. One minute things are good, the next somebody dies or gets sick or stops being your friend. You can't count on anyone or anything, which makes life difficult if you're a planner.

Actually, that's the best part of tonight. I know exactly what's ahead of me. Planning it, anticipating its finality and precision, is the best sedative I've ever taken.

How did I come up with my plan?

It came to me a little over six months ago. One night

I dreamed I was in a plane flying toward the milky blue lining that separates the earth's atmosphere from space. It looked like a little square of heaven itself from the airplane window. The me in the dream was thinking, *God must be there*. The flight lasted forever as we hurled ever closer to space but never actually left our atmosphere. There were no other passengers on board the plane. The cabin was empty of attendants, and all the storage cabinets were flung open and empty. The captain's voice came on repeatedly, asking flight attendants to prepare for landing. The plane flew higher and higher and began to shake—just a bit at first, then faster—but I did not scream and I wasn't scared. In the dream, I was constantly cinching my seat belt while I watched that horizon of milky blue heaven before me, just out of reach. I felt safe, like when I was a happy little kid before everything changed, before my father killed himself. It felt like the plane was just going to coast like this forever, and then suddenly the plane dropped into a downward spiral back toward the earth and I tried to scream, but no sound came out. Just before impact, everything turned to black.

I woke up breathless and in a cold sweat, alone in my room, still weighted with the haziness of sedation. (I probably should have mentioned that the day before my dream, I had had another "incident" and they had loaded me up on sedatives to keep me calm.) It was as though God, or someone or something, had delivered a message through my dream: no more "incidents." In my heart, I knew the first and second "incidents" were halfhearted, non-attempts at hitting the switch. That's why I'd never let the doctors tell me otherwise. Suicide requires true intentions, and mine never were. The first time, I wanted my mother to find me with the carving knife and I wanted her to cry and bemoan my fate, like she did my father's and grandmother's. But I never intended to die that day. The second, well, let's just say, some of the staff got a chuckle out of my lame efforts. But they won't be laughing tomorrow morning, and they won't think my efforts were without genius.

I come from a family of depressives and suicidals, beginning with my great-grandfather, then my grandmother, and then my father. At the time of my first incident, I desired the specialness their lives took on after they offed themselves, how everyone talked endlessly about their struggles and their dramatic ends, but I didn't know then if I had the courage to follow their path. The first two dry runs told me I did and that I just needed a plan that didn't allow me to be saved.

When I woke from my dream, I knew I had found one. I knew exactly what I had to do in order to escape Life House and my miserable, painful existence.

It was simple, so simple. I remember a little smile sneaking onto my face, feeling conscious of my muscles stretching in unfamiliar ways. It surprised me, the joy of knowing, of planning it. I still don't know why I had never thought of it before. But I started working on my plan that morning and it was as grand and simple as any other.

I would be good. I'd be great. I'd be better than any patient ever stuck inside the walls of Life House. I'd smile; I'd talk; I'd comfort; I'd reveal; I'd comply. And I'd compile enough points to earn a trip home. It didn't matter if the trip home was for a week. Once on board the plane, I'd be free: of doctors, nurses, attendants, patients, my mother, my memories, anxieties, and fears. Free to move about the cabin. Free to enter the bathroom and lock the door and pill myself to nowhere. Free to die. Free to live in oblivion.

As I lay in my bed that morning six months ago, I knew I had stumbled on a plan that would work.

Chapter 3

"Hi, my name is Jane Solis. I'm flying home."

I'm standing at the nurses' station at Life House. I have a couple of things I need to do before I can get on my flight. *Five hours and thirty-seven minutes.*

Every time I look at my father's watch, my stomach flip-flops, but I can't help myself. My body is in a state of perpetual contradiction, alive with anticipation and simultaneously dead of all other emotion. The desire to see this through is propelling me forward, but inside I am cold and dead like a slow-breathing fish hoping somebody cuts my head off. *Stay upbeat and positive, Jane. Upbeat and positive, all day long.* That's what I keep telling myself over and over.

First, I need to pick up my pass to leave campus.

Hence, my stop at the nurses' station. Second, I need to have one last session with Old Doctor, who never misses a damn appointment. His unflagging punctuality and reliability bug me even though I think that's why he gets me so well. I'm sure he counts the minutes too. (He wears two watches; what's that about?) As usual, I'm dreading our conversation. What if he figures me out? What if he's been waiting this whole time to expose me? *Stop the thoughts, Jane. Upbeat and positive.*

"What a pretty name," says the nurse, a ragged-looking woman in a white uniform. She's new, or substituting over the holidays. Her name tag says *Nancy C.* That's common around here; it makes me think the staff don't want any of us to know their full names. I don't blame them. No telling what some of us might do when we get out.

Nancy C. is overweight, with an inch of gray roots showing at the part of her blond hair, but she has warm green eyes and is trying hard to connect with me.

"Jane Solis," she tries again, "that's a name that belongs in lights."

She spins in her chair and types my name into her computer. I look above her at a glass-covered print of Cézanne's *Apples* and I see my reflection hovering there like a ghost. My brown hair hangs ragged over my shoulders. It was shaved short when I arrived. Now it's an unkempt mess of waves and half curls. My slate-gray eyes are barely visible against their pearly backdrop, but they are haunting nonetheless. I never look in mirrors anymore, so my reflection seems much older than what I remember. That's such a weird thing to think. I am worn thin around the cheeks, like death is creeping up from inside me. It spooks me, and I let out a tiny yelp.

Nancy wheels her chair around to the filing cabinets and pulls out a pass. She gives me a long stare. I look down, annoyed by how much I'm slipping in these last few hours. *Pull it together, Jane.*

The printer spits out a card with my name and a thousand different numbers and symbols, and she signs her name on the back and then tucks it into a laminated pocket that has a lanyard attached to it. She hands it to me and tells me not to lose it.

"Thanks."

"Have you left campus before? Do you need a review about how to get to the airport bus? Do you need any special assistance, Jane?"

"Yes, I mean no, I don't."

"You know the rules, right? Until you reach Newark Airport, and are in your mother's care, you are still under our supervision. You have a pass to use the hospital bus to and from town. From there you will take the airport bus at Grove and Main Street in town to the airport. You don't need to take any other transportation, and your supervisor will place you on that airport bus. If for any reason you miss the bus or get separated or even just get nervous, there's a number on the back of the card. Don't hesitate to use it."

I have had all of this explained to me at least three times, but I nod pleasantly.

"While you're in town, you need to adhere to the rules of your sobriety pledge, obviously, and check in with your supervisor about your plans."

I nod again. "Yes, ma'am."

She looks me up and down for a second. She's assessing my state of mind, like I'm poised to freak out or something. She'll never see that in me. I'm pure ice. Planners are that way. If we have time—and I've had six months—we can pretty much fool anybody. Sure, I have my tics too, minor personal habits the docs like to label and acronym to death. Christ, I think everybody here has them. But that's just my anxiety run wild, like my constant watch-watching and my time obsession and all. If I let it, it could grind everything to a halt. But my plan keeps it all in check.

"Will I have time to shop for a present for my mother before I get on the bus to the airport?"

For example, a little talk is always the bow on top of

the present when it comes to deceiving a nurse or attendant. They get wrapped up in the chatty minutia and become blind to what is standing before them. In this case, a patient who is planning to hit the switch. The nurse studies a sheet on her desk.

"Yes, it looks like you should have about a half hour, but just make sure you check in with your supervisor and carry your pass with you wherever you go." She reaches into a drawer.

"And here's a cell phone."

I already knew this drill, but she told me anyway.

"It only calls this number, and you are to use it if something goes wrong or you need some help. See, just press this button. We'll be right here. You enjoy yourself, Jane. Merry Christmas shopping!" she says with a big smile.

"You too," I say inanely, and she smiles, a little too hard for my liking. I wonder if she suspects something. Did I give something away?

Chapter 4

I walk back to my room, head down as I pass Old Doctor's morning Group session. It's nearly ten-fifty and I only have ten minutes to get everything ready before my final session with him.

As I approach my room, I feel my lungs seize up. My breath rushes out. It feels like all my blood has dropped to my toes and suddenly I'm a little dizzy, enough so that I put my hand on the wall for a second. If I hyperventilate, and it wouldn't be the first time, they will never let me get on that airplane. *Steady, Jane.*

I look back over to Group, which is breaking up, and watch Old Doctor, who is giving his full attention to a private discussion he's having with BS. I close my eyes and concentrate on taking one very deep breath. Then another:

in through the nose, out through the mouth. And I feel my body settle down and the dizziness dissipate.

I pull my hand from the wall and slip into my room and stuff my travel bag with the essentials. Obviously I have no need for a travel bag, but I don't want to be found out by a nosy nurse: "If she's going home for a week, why'd she leave all her stuff here? Doesn't she need a bag? Red alert, put out an APB!" They are trained to spot that kind of shit, but I've trained myself not to give them anything to spin their wheels about. In five hours and seven minutes, I'll have won that battle.

I look around my room and nausea swirls in my stomach. The pink comforter my mother gave me for the winters lies wrinkled and wasted on my bed, full of old sweat and sad energy. Why does every depressive bed always look the same?

I feel a bead of sweat trickle down my back. *Nerves,* I tell myself. *Buck up and buckle down, Jane.*

I look at my window, where I have spent endless hours in manic thoughts about the time I was wasting here at Life House. I walk over to the night table and pull open the drawer and take out a photo of me and my father at Christmastime.

Nobody knows I have this photo. I took it from one of my mother's photo albums. She has millions of photos all over the house, and mostly I hate them all. I've told her this, and during check-in at the hospital I made a point to tell Old Doctor this in front of her. It made her sniffle, which made me feel sad inside but smile on the outside.

I hold the photo up. I love his face. His skin was olive and smooth, and his eyes were chocolate brown. A big sob rises in my throat, so I kiss Dad's face, and a tear drops onto the glossy finish. I quickly wipe it off and place the photo on the bottom of my bag.

Nurses or not, I do need a few things. A pad of paper to write my mother a goodbye note. I'll tuck it between the netting and upright tray table on the back of the seat in front of me.

I need my wallet to get from town to the airport and to get my plane ticket from the automated ticket machine. My mother bought the ticket on a credit card and mailed the credit card to the hospital. It was given to me with great ceremony yesterday. "Jane, this is for the pickup of your ticket only—your mother is bestowing great trust in you, and I think you've earned it." *Oh yes I have, with every lie and fake tear you swallowed, sir. Don't worry, Dr. Gallus, going wild with a credit card isn't in my plans.*

I open my wallet. I have a hundred bucks in cash. (Money my mother gave me to use, *just in case*.) I pull my dad's watch from my pocket and check the time. Three minutes to my last session.

What am I going to say to him? It has to be perfect because Old Doctor isn't stupid. If he catches a whiff of the Plan or of anything out of whack, I'm done. No pass. No flight. No oblivion. But if I can give him a faux revelation that's not too big, but not too small, he'll get happy and animated with his own genius and forget about me. He's human, after all. Notebooks out, people: This is how you can fool all adult beings. Make them think they are genius. They are even more vain than we are.

And, frankly, I'm not a genius myself but I am a very good liar.

Chapter 5

"Jane?" Old Doctor says.

I hear him, but I want to move on. He wants to discuss my father. What I remember of him during the holidays. I've been barfing out my usual responses for more than twenty minutes: I was only eleven, and he died on Christmas Eve. Of course, "died" isn't right. It is like me saying "incident" about my *incident*, I suppose, but I'd never tell Old Doctor that. *Died* is what you say about people who go, gently or not, into that good night propelled by some external force: cancerous cells or a speeding car. My father called his own shot. He hit his own switch, as the patients here at Life House are fond of saying. My father killed himself. (That's how Old Doctor would want me to say it, with honesty and frankness.)

"I remember very little about his death," I say, which is both true and untrue, but to say anything else now, after all my half memories told and untold over the past year, would raise too many questions. And I know why he is asking. It's because I'm going home and it's Christmas and inevitably things will be stirred up. That's what the holidays are for me: a big stir-up-shit festival. People don't get this, but memories are just like the future. You can't plan for when they show up, and you've got no control over them when they do. Worst of all, the older you get, the sadder they are. At least, that's been my experience.

And by the way, nobody stirs the shit like my mother. That's what Old Doctor is probably biting his nails about late at night. He's met my mother, so he knows. She's bonkersville with all the photographs in every fucking room, like having a picture in your room will keep your dead husband alive in your heart. It certainly keeps the depression alive and kicking in mine. Leaving the house, of course, isn't an option either. For instance, if you go shopping at the Stop and Shop, a banal act by any sane person's account, every aisle is the location of a forgotten memory. "Oh, your father loved Honey Nut Cheerios," or, "Coffee, your father just loved the aroma of a freshly brewed cup." Really, Mom? Did he like the soft feel of Charmin toilet paper too? It's enough to make you want to scream, "If he loved so much, why the fuck did he kill himself!"

I hear Old Doc clear gravel from his throat.

"Sorry. What did you ask?" I say, looking to buy time.

Old Doctor sits in his big leather chair and waits for me to continue. His arms are thin and knotted with bones that threaten to poke right out of his saggy, chapped skin.

"You haven't been home in a year," he says, switching gears on me. "How does it make you feel?"

"I'm ready," I say, but offer nothing else.

"Ready?" he finally asks, after waiting a few moments.

I worry for a second that the combination of my reluctance to speak and my short, unproductive answers will lead to his questioning my readiness. I look down at my shoes, pretending to ponder his question deeply. *I can't die in these shoes.* They're old lady shoes my mom bought for me in case Life House had a prom or something. Think about that for a second, and you have a little window into what I'm dealing with. My mom figured there might be some nice boys I could dance with here at this fine mental institution.

I should be clear: I don't blame my mom for anything that happened. My dad was a suicide seeker, like his mom was and I'd bet her mom or dad was too. I'm sure there are studies that show this better than I can state it, but if somebody in your family has killed themselves, you are way more likely to try it yourself. I do blame her for not letting go and letting his ugly decision fester like an open sore on my life: left untreated, it can become a problem, as doctors like to say. And I guess I've become the problem. Sure, she took me to doctors galore, but she could never fucking move on, so that's why we're stuck in the same place since the Offing on that Christmas five years ago.

"You keep looking at your shoes. Why?"

"My mother gave them to me in case there was an event here. A dance or something. God, it sounds so pathetic to say it out loud. She's bonkers, right?"

He nods again, more acknowledgement than agreement. But I say nothing. Finally, he relents.

"Is your trip home an event?"

I feel it. Those old bony hands have taken hold of something inside of me. But did he know what he had his hands on?

"Sadly, a bus trip to a podunk town, followed by another bus to a sad little airport in a hick city is a big event in my life these days." I crack a nervous smile. I don't like where this is going.

He looks at me, waiting. He wants me to barf my secret plan onto the table.

I sit stone-faced.

He leans in, focusing on my eyes, trying to tighten his grip on the unknown inside of me. I bet the use of the word *event* has pricked his antennae and he's searching for his prize. *Show no emotion, Jane.*

"Jane," he says softly.

I notice for the first time that I'm shaking. He must see a little opening because his eyes twinkle. I have to say something to break his spell.

"I hate these shoes. My mother likes to buy shoes. I hate her fucking shoes. My father made fun of her shoes. I remember that." Stop talking, Jane. No more.

I look down at my shoes, and surprisingly a tear hits them. I wish I could say that the waterworks are an act, part of my small revelation, but they are beyond my control. This old bastard has a way with the questions, and with the timing of them, I suppose. I've been so busy blocking knowledge of the Plan from Old Doctor, my other secrets have become less defended. Or maybe I'm nervous about today. It feels like something inside of me is breaking open.

"Why did he make fun of her?"

"I have no idea. He's been dead for so long. He used to say she had 'more shoes than a princess.' He liked ties. My mother and I always bought him two ties every Christmas.

We'd open a pile of gifts: toys for me, shoe boxes for Mom, and Daddy would always open two thin tie boxes."

I stop talking for a moment and visualize my father in my mind's eye. I always see the same picture when I try to remember what he looked like: what he was actually like day to day. He's sitting in his studio, leaning back in his chair staring out the window. I'd walk in very quietly, thinking that he had no idea I was sneaking into his studio—but he always knew. I was a tiny little girl then, maybe five or six. He'd say, "Hey pumpkin, can I have a pumpkin seed?" and I'd always say, "For what purpose, sir!"—it was a line he'd taught me. "I'd like to roast and toast it and eat it all up." And I'd shake my head no with a little impish grin. He'd fake being offended and plead and plead for a pumpkin seed until I laughed. Then he'd scoop me up and kiss my head and tell me he loved me over and over.

It's funny because the day before he died, he walked up to me in the TV room where I was sitting and watching an old movie called *The House Without a Christmas Tree*. He leaned over and kissed the top of my head, like he did when I was five. But now I was eleven, and I turned around and shouted at him, "Don't do that! It's weird. Don't kiss the top of my head or touch my hair." He kind of stood there frozen for a second and then smiled. He said, "Sorry, pumpkin, I didn't mean to bother you."

"You're not bothering me—just don't kiss the top of my head anymore."

He nodded okay and said, "I'm sorry, pumpkin," and left. The next morning he was dead. I never got to say sorry or anything or explain it. *I* didn't hate it—just my eleven-year-old self hated it. That's what eleven-year-olds do. I hate thinking about that and that's why I hate thinking about him too much as well. But everybody always wants to talk about it.

"My mother saved his ties. I won't look at them or her stupid pictures of him. His studio is like a creepy shrine or mausoleum. It makes me sick. She makes me sick. I love her, but she makes me sick. All she wants to do is keep everything exactly the way it was, except it isn't. He's dead. And I'm crazy now too, just like he was." This was exhausting me. Not the way I wanted to spend this last session.

"You'll see your mother tomorrow. Perhaps we can have her fly back with you and we can have a family discussion about the photos and ties, and about your father's office, if it is upsetting to you. Each of you listening to the other might be helpful."

There's a long pause again and he patiently waits for me to respond. But I sit stone-faced. He gazes at me for a few minutes, which makes me really uncomfortable, until finally I blurt out the first thing that comes to mind.

"I've never spent Christmas without her. It made me feel lonely to think about that. I'm flying home. I'm glad about that. It'll be like old times. We can talk then; there's no need for her to come here."

He nods, hoping to keep me talking.

"I want to go shopping with her. It's a happy memory for me."

Then there's a long pause where I say nothing and he sits there like a statue in a park waiting for the nut job on the bench to talk.

"You will; I'm sure."

He grabs a box of tissues.

I take one. I cry.

He looks at his clock, then says, "You have a bus to catch."

I sniffle and smile.

"Have a wonderful trip, Jane. Remember this: No matter how dark your time at home gets, you are not alone. There might be a moment or even a day or two that feels that way, where you are thinking, 'no one in the world can see or hear me,' but it isn't true. We are always with you. We believe in you. And you can reach out and check in with us by phone at any time."

I wonder if that's his subconscious at work. If he's worried that something bad might happen. I wonder if that notion will blossom in his head and if he'll try to come and save me as I'm getting on the plane. *Magical thinking,* I chide myself.

"Merry Christmas, Jane."

Chapter 6

I grab my bag from my room and ditch the old lady dance shoes. I slide on my snow boots and pull the bottoms of my jeans down over the top of them. I tuck my white blouse into my jeans and pull on a dark brown V-neck sweater and then my winter jacket. I hurry downstairs to the lobby. After flashing the bus pass hanging around my neck, I line up behind four other patients from the addiction floor, none of whom I know. It's five minutes before noon and the bus is already idling in front of the institute. I loathe it.

It's a short yellow bus, with the words LIFE HOUSE printed along the side in large block letters. They might as well have written NUT HOUSE, just to be sure that everyone who saw us in town knew who we were. We all walk onto the bus like the medicated zombies we are, eyes looking anywhere but at each other. An attendant checks our names off and the bus slides into gear.

I check my watch: three hours, fifty-seven minutes till takeoff. I close my eyes and imagine that milky blue sky above the earth. *Almost there, Jane.*

As I step off the bus, I check my watch. It's only 12:20 p.m., so I've got a good forty minutes before the airport bus departs. So far so good—in the time department, that is.

The good townspeople of Powder River stare at us like we're losers. Who wouldn't? A busload of adolescent nut jobs pulls into your town for a little Yuletide shopping and cheer and your jaw isn't hitting the floor?

I stand there for a few seconds, momentarily unsure of myself. The attendant, her name is May, notices my indecision.

"Jane, your bus picks you up right here in just about thirty minutes. Are you okay? Do you want me to stand here with you?"

"No," I say. Then, "I want to buy my mother a gift, from Powder River."

"Would you like me to come with you?"

I shake my head no. "That's okay. Do I have time?"

"I think so; you should be back here in twenty minutes

to be safe." She pauses, then continues, "You look very worried, Jane. Are you sure everything is all right? I think your mom will understand if you don't have something."

"I'm fine," I mumble. "I want to buy a tie for my father, too." She is just an outsourced attendant; she doesn't know my father put a hole in his head on Christmas Eve, so the lie doesn't register. But what if she tells Old Doctor or one of the nurses who know me? Note to self: You are becoming self-destructive. Stick to the Plan.

"Well, there's Lila's Vintage a few blocks up on the corner," she says. "They should have ties. I'll come with you."

"Thank you, but I'm really fine."

She looks at me, and her mind is calculating all that could go wrong and weighing it against what is the good and right thing to do at Christmas.

"Okay, but you don't have a lot of time. To be safe, be back in fifteen minutes."

I nod and turn, walking into a whipping cold wind. Slush, salt, and sand cover the sidewalk and the freezing temperatures have made everything slick. Despite the cold, there are people milling about, looking in shop windows, and a dozen or so kids from a local choir are assembled outside Town Hall singing carols. An old-fashioned black pot hangs from a stand in front of the choir and little kids take turns tossing in their mothers' coins.

I still feel the attendant's eyes on my back, so I turn around, but she has disappeared. Where has she gone? *She's not calling the institute. Don't be paranoid.* I look carefully on the far corners of each side of the street. Nothing. She's shopping, like everyone else. *Don't be crazy, Jane.*

I push into the wind, past the door to Lila's Vintage and into Dowden's Drugstore on the far corner. An old man with a short white pharmacist's jacket looks up from his perch and gives me a cursory smile before returning to his business, counting pills.

From the back entrance to the store, a FedEx man walks in carrying a handful of packages and brings them to the counter.

As the two men chat, I examine a display of hand-knitted mittens and hats. Candy canes dance in a pattern on the woven yarn: red and white, green and red, black and pink. It's not as much a part of the Plan as the cold medicines and sleeping pills, but the more items I bring to the counter, the less likely the pharmacist might be to question why a teenage girl needs such a weird combination of over-the-counter medications. I pull a hat and a pair of mittens off the rack, tucking my old ones into my pockets. I slip the mittens on. They're warm and fuzzy. I grab a couple pairs of each: one for Mom and one for Dad, just in case the attendant asks.

I walk down one of the aisles and nab a pair of sunglasses, large and black. I put them on and look in the mirror. I look like a bug. I like it.

In the next aisle, I find the cold medicines and sleeping pills. I pull down the bottles needed for the specific combination I researched online. I walk toward the pharmacist and place all of my items on the counter. He rings me up, and I hand him cash.

"Thank you, dear. Come again."

He hands me a bag with my "medicine" and a separate bag with my new sunglasses and the extra mittens and hat. I put on my glasses and drop the drug bag into my travel bag. I walk to the door and disappear onto the street.

I check the time. It is twelve forty-five. Fifteen minutes to spare. Three hours and fifteen minutes until takeoff.

Chapter 7

"**D**id you find what you were looking for?" May greets me as I return to the corner. She must have been concerned that I might run or get lost. I don't like that she has me on her mind. *Play it cool, Jane.*

"No, but I found mittens and stuff for my mom and dad."

I open the bag and show her the mittens and hat.

"Those are cute—you got them at Dowden's?"

I look down at the white paper bag and notice the little Dowden's logo on it. *Damn it, Jane. You want to blow this. That's becoming clear.*

"I didn't like what Lila's had. It all smelled of mothballs."

The attendant smiles and says, "I'm not much of a vintage gal myself. You know, Dowden's isn't on the list, Jane."

"Can that be our secret?" I say, with the deftness of a lifetime liar at the peak of her game. "I wasn't thinking about that when I went in; it was just close by and I wanted to get back here in time." I pause for a minute, searching her face, which is unreadable.

"I'm not a substance abuser, you know," I add in a rush. "That's not my bag; you could check my records. Really. I know it's important not to be late, too."

She smiles, nods, and winks at me.

We make small talk after that and exchange our family Christmas rituals. She's from a don't-open-presents-until-morning family and we are a blow-your-brains-out-before-morning family, so we didn't have a lot in common. I lie, of course, and say we are also never-before-morning present openers. Blah blah blah.

Before I get on the bus, I give her an impromptu hug, which she returns. It makes her feel special and, hopefully, that will seal her silence. She likes me now and we have a secret; she'll never turn me in, right?

It's only five after one when the bus pulls out of Powder River. I sit in the back, which looks weird because I'm one of only three people on the bus. *Be normal, Jane. Just do normal things.*

My heart starts to pound fast, my lungs seize up a bit, and I wonder if the woman five rows ahead of me can hear it and if she suspects why I'm here. *Nobody knows about the Plan*, I tell myself. *I'm just a girl flying home to New Jersey. I'm not from Life House. How could they tell?* I look myself up and down. Nothing out of the ordinary. Nothing at all.

The bus rolls through town and then hits the highway to the airport. I see a rabbit dash across the snow, and I wonder how big the world must seem through those eyes. Or if the landscape is seriously abbreviated because he's so low to the ground. Or maybe the rabbit can't see very far at all and therefore nothing matters. I'll never know; I can't look it up at home. My mind races a million miles per hour. I am driving myself bonkers, so I close my eyes, steady my breath, and imagine the deep, blue-black horizon I'll be seeing through the airplane window. Slowly, I feel a sense of relief and quiet wash through me. *I am so close now,* I tell myself over and over.

Twenty minutes more and we are at the airport. It's one fifty-eight, two minutes ahead of schedule. My heartbeat slows. My mind clears. I can taste oblivion.

I walk off the bus with determination and more confidence than I've felt in years. It is a kind of euphoria, and I remind myself to ignore its siren—it is not a feeling I can hold on to. It only exists because I am preparing to execute the Plan. *Nothing more complicated than that—don't let your mind play tricks on you, Jane.* I felt this feeling before my first "incident." *Don't believe for a second this is a feeling you can sustain. This is your body trying to trick your mind into giving up the Plan.*

Chapter 8

The Boise Airport is tiny, with just a handful of runways, a totally different species compared with Newark or Kennedy. Holiday travelers bustle from ticketing over to the main gate, and arrivals move from the main gate to ground transportation. It's a little beehive of activity and a lot busier than I imagined. Somehow that's comforting; it makes me feel invisible.

I head directly to West Air. As I walk, I feel a buzzing in my bag. I look in and pull out the Life House cell phone. It's lit up with the general number to Life House. I debate for a second about answering it, but then decide against it. If they're trying to reach me, it can't be good. *Why did you have to show off to the attendant, Jane?* I pinch my leg hard, just to give myself a reminder about screwing up anymore.

I look up at the departure board and I see a long list of canceled departures, beginning at 5 p.m. My flight's status is still on time. There must be a storm coming through. Damn it. Damn it. My heart starts to race and I swear to myself about how much I hate life and the unexpected and how if God will just get me on a plane, I promise I won't go through with the Plan. I'm lying, of course, but frankly, if I thought God paid attention to the details, I probably wouldn't be here in the first place. I put my mother's credit card into the ticketing machine and it prints my boarding pass. Boarding at 3:30 p.m. Thank you, God!

Before I can go to gate 12, I have to pass through security. They have two scanners for the whole airport, and the thought of missing my flight makes me break into a sweat. I check my watch; it's still only two twenty. *I'll be fine,* I tell myself.

There's a line of about ten people waiting to be processed. A young guy with a punkish haircut and a snowboard is having trouble passing through the right-side scanner. He probably has a metal plate in his head from falling off a ramp. I could just kill him. He looks at me as if to say, "Sorry—it isn't me." He's cute, but really annoying right now.

Behind him, there is a group of rock climbers who all wear T-shirts that say *Matternaught: Avalanche Valley,*

Grand Tetons. They are surrounded by a massive amount of baggage and gear.

They are loud and boisterous, like they are not used to congregating in crowded public places. They simply prove to me what I've always thought: there isn't a group of people in the world that doesn't bug me, given the right time and circumstances.

I check my watch again. It's already two thirty. My anxiety is causing me to bite down on the inside of my cheek to avoid screaming right now.

A newlywed couple stands directly in front of me, waiting to go through the left scanner. Their names are Margaret and Eddie, two of the many facts I've gleaned from their unusually loud conversation. I never had any particular issues with the newly married, but now I begin to radiate contempt in their direction. Their incessant, narcissistic conversation about themselves is enough to make me vomit. I bite down harder on my cheek and I taste the salty metallic flavors in my own blood.

Margaret is complaining about her wedding ring; "Eddie, it's just so heavy, it makes my wrist tired." Eddie looks proud and embarrassed all at once and says, "You may have to start working out, Margaret . . . heh heh heh."

They keep up this nauseating chatter, all interspersed with unnecessary touching until they kiss goodbye before

Margaret passes through the scanner without Eddie. Then they both get teary and actually blow each other kisses. I want to scream, but I keep my head down and know I'll be thirty-five-thousand feet in the air soon enough.

After Margaret walks through, I approach the scanner, but the TSA officer puts his hand up to stop me and asks the punk rocker to walk through my scanner. I explode with anxiety and shout, "My flight is leaving soon!"

I must have screamed really loudly because the immediate area goes still and both the snowboarder and the TSA officer turn around.

The TSA officer looks me up and down and assesses my level of crazy. Is it Christmas crazy or real crazy? That's what he's trying to determine.

"Miss, what time is your flight?"

"Four."

He checks his watch and looks at me strangely. "You have an hour and a half, miss. I suggest you take a deep breath and calm yourself down."

I bite down harder as I nod and now I'm swallowing blood.

The snowboarder picks up his bag and his board and moves a few feet to the side. I can't help looking at him. He is stone cold, completely devoid of emotion. His cheekbones are sharp, like they were carved from rock.

"It's cool," he says. "Let her go."

I nod thanks, mostly because I can't open my mouth. I put up my hands and pass through the scanner and body check. No alarms go off, so I guess there's no detector for somebody who's planning to do bodily harm to herself.

I grab my bag from the tray and walk quickly to the first restroom, where I lock myself in a stall and spit out a little blood into the toilet from where I bit my own mouth. I can barely breathe, so I sit down and cover my mouth with my hands, trying to limit the air coming in and out of my lungs. It works. I gather myself and splash some water on my face from the sink. I look at myself in the mirror and am alarmed at the high color in my cheeks. *Calm down,* I order myself before I walk back out.

I make my way to gate 12 and find a seat. I check the time. Two forty-five. I look at the flight board and pray again that my flight doesn't get canceled.

I check my watch again, just out of habit; it is still two forty-five. I wonder if I can make it another forty-five minutes. I slide my tongue between my teeth and clamp down. Not too hard, not enough to bleed, but just enough to focus my mind and clear my head. *I'm gonna make it.* I say it over and over.

Chapter 9

To my relief, West Air actually has their shit together. They board us early and prepare us to lift off early if the controllers will allow it. My seat is three rows from the back and I have a window seat.

I make my way back without incident and without really making eye contact with anybody, including the attendant, whom I naturally don't trust.

A couple of climbers with large bags come down the aisle, and I pray they don't sit next to me. They stop in the row in front of me and start unloading their stuff. It's a lot. And there's a lot of loud and tedious discussion about a green duffle bag that won't fit in the overhead compartment, which is finally resolved by stuffing it, with a lot of force, under a seat. Then the captain comes on and asks the flight attendants to prepare the cabin for takeoff.

I finally breathe a sigh of relief: to have a row to myself is simply too good to be true. Then, at the last moment before takeoff, there's a commotion at the front of the plane. The seat next to me is still empty, though many others are as well. I start muttering to myself, "Please don't sit next to me, please don't sit next to me, please don't sit next to me." But God giveth and He taketh away.

I look up and find the snowboard punker looming over my row in the aisle. He folds himself into the seat next to mine. I see that he's even younger than I thought, now that we are face-to-face.

"Sorry, I don't fit very well," he apologizes after stepping on my bag and elbowing me on his way down into his seat.

"No worries," I say so quietly I don't think he hears me.

I turn away, fingering the netting on the back of the seat in front of me.

The captain comes on shortly after and asks flight attendants to take their seats. I take a deep breath. My dream, my plan is coming true. Some minor bumps and a little anxiety, but I'm on the runway. I smile to myself and look sideways to make sure skate-punk guy didn't see me.

The plane taxis to the runway, stops, and then does a

one-eighty. It slowly picks up speed again, and then the engines roar to life. The g-force pulls me back into my seat and we zip down the runway. I turn to the window and mumble a prayer to God to watch over my flight. It's instinct, and even as I say it, I know how ridiculous I am. I'm about to hit my own switch and I'm praying for a safe takeoff.

Whenever I fly, I say the same prayer. I call to the dead before me: my father, my grandfather and grandmother, a cousin I only knew one summer who has since died of an infection in his gallbladder, and my English teacher, Miss Lathrop, who had a seizure and choked on a ham sandwich. She died alone in her apartment. It is my private parade of dead angels, and I ask them to carry the wings of the plane, to take me home. I guess I'm asking them to carry me far enough along so I can take my life. Miss Lathrop would have said, "How ironic." I always wonder what she was thinking just before she died.

The plane skips up and then bends steeply to the left. We hold the trajectory for about ten to fifteen minutes, and then we level off.

"Paul Hart, Cambridge, Mass.," my neighbor says, extending his hand. He has a muted New England accent and is trim with strong, wiry muscles in his forearms. I accept his hand automatically, but frowning, and withdraw mine almost immediately. His hands are big and rough with calluses.

"They used to be softer."

"What?"

"My hands. I hadn't realized how calloused they got until right now." He nods at my soft, pale hands. "I guess you weren't here for the climbing."

I glare at him. He stares back, and we just kind of gaze at each other in a very awkward way. There's an insult or an assumption in what he just said. I have no idea whether he meant to be rude or if he's sort of an idiot, but I feel my eyes welling up, so I look down.

"Everything okay?" he asks.

"I didn't mean anything," he assures me, "just an observation."

I look up, having regained my composure. He has thick brown hair and his face is cherubic except for the dark stubble that sandpapers his chin. I can hear the relentless beating of some punk band that probably nobody but he and his snowboard buddies know tinning out from his unplugged earplugs. Annoyingly, he's still wearing his sunglasses.

"I saw you say a prayer there," he says, withdrawing a bit as he organizes himself in his seat. His voice sounds like gravel. He's probably a smoker. "I hope you have wings; it looks like there's a huge storm coming."

He laughs a little at his own joke and removes his sunglasses. Baby blues, no surprise—all the jerks have them. I wonder if everything that comes out of his mouth is annoying or if I would find anything anyone did annoying at this moment. I decide it is probably just Paul Hart.

"Yes. God is dead and all that," I say a little more abruptly than I intended.

"What?" he says. "I don't understand."

I realize I was having a conversation in my head that was about three responses ahead of Paul's innocuous quip. I tend to do that—imagine conversations before they happen. That's why people sometimes have a tough time understanding me and I them. But Paul's a bright one and catches up quickly.

"I bet you're a philosophy major," he says, if not a tad smugly. "I get it."

"Yes, how did you know?" I say. It is very difficult for me not to lie in a situation like this. It just feels safer. I open my mouth to lie more, but I am too tired, too anxious, and I will myself to stop.

He looks at me strangely. "I think they're all full of shit. They don't know anything more about life than you do."

I take in his face for a moment. I can see where he will grow old, where the crinkles will carve a path from the corner of his eyes. I bet he's a worrier. I bet he's a fronter—

all bravado up front and a squirming mass of anxiety underneath.

"Right," I say, picking up the emergency information card and studying it.

He looks at me for a second and then a crooked smile opens his face. He thinks I'm a bitch. Or just not worth the trouble. He puts on his headphones, pushes his sunglasses back on, and leans back in his seat.

I put on my headphones too, close my eyes, and turn away. I hope he doesn't try talking to me again. I listen to him rustling through his bag and adjusting his seat belt. There's a lot of show in it, like he's trying to get my attention, but I resist, which is not so much a part of the Plan but more my nature. Show-offs repulse me.

The captain comes on: "Folks, I'm sorry for the abrupt departure this evening, but Control wanted us out before the runway got snowed in. There's a bit of a storm ahead of us, so I'm going to have the seat belt sign on for the duration while we try to stay a step ahead of it. We'll be heading a bit farther north than we normally do, but we should right our course just past this front and land in Chicago as scheduled. So please cooperate and try to stay in your seat if possible. Thank you for making the choice to fly West Air, and enjoy your trip."

"Dude, where would we be going?" Paul says loudly.

He looks to me with that crooked smile I've now come to despise. Is he talking to me? Or is he responding to the captain? I do not look at him. I pull the blanket from the netting in the seat in front of me and wrap myself up in it. I close my eyes and wait. *One more unexpected benefit of the Plan,* I think. *I'll never hear this Masshole's accent again.*

Chapter 10

Unbelievably, I nodded off. Or, I guess I did, because when I open my eyes, the lights are out except for a few reading lights in front. The plane is mostly empty, so it looks like a ghost town in here. Paul is asleep with a map propped on his stomach. His book is tucked underneath his elbow.

I check my watch, and it is after five. I look into my bag and pull out my pad of paper. I've thought about this note forever. I steady the pad, but there's some turbulence and it makes it difficult to write. Thankfully, what I have to say is very brief.

Dear Mom,
I'm going with Dad. I'll see you on the other

side. Don't blame yourself. I was born with it and there's nothing to be done.

Love,
Jane

I fold it up and write MOM on the front. I tuck it into the netting of the seat in front of me. I try to place it where somebody will find it, but I am suddenly overwhelmed by a fear that the letter will go unnoticed and my mother won't ever read it. That she'll go through the rest of her life blaming herself for my death. I stare at it awhile, then take the letter and stuff it into my pants pocket. I unfasten my seat belt and turn so I'm facing the seat and Paul and then step over him, balancing myself until I can lift my back leg over. He stirs for a moment but does not wake.

The bathroom sits directly behind me. I check my watch, and it's forty-five minutes since takeoff, which is cutting it close. If I dose now, by the time we land in Chicago, I should be gone. A brief shiver runs down my spine as I imagine myself clinging to life and being wheeled on a gurney through O'Hare airport. That must be hell. *Focus on the now, Jane.*

The lone flight attendant is sitting at the front of the plane, flipping through a magazine, probably relieved that the turbulence means she doesn't have to wheel the drinks cart down the aisle filling orders like a waitress. Finally an element of the Plan comes to fruition. I open the bath-room door and step in. I push the bolt lock and close the door. I turn and sit on the toilet. I put my face in my hands and wonder what my mother is doing now. I cry a little, not because I'm afraid, but because I am so relieved to be here and at the same time I am sad for my mother. Something will happen to her when she hears this, something perma-nent. I feel sad about it, but it's not enough to stop me.

I dip into my bag and pull out my pills. One by one, I press them through the blister packaging. The bumpi-ness of the flight makes it difficult, but I manage to fill a small white paper cup with what I'll need. I pull another cup from the metal sleeve and fill it from the tiny sink. I steady myself.

I say my takeoff prayer again and hope my angels will carry me home. *What works for one flight should work for all*, I tell myself. I open my mouth and reach for the pills. The plane hits an air bump and jumps up and down. I quickly put my other hand against the wall and steady myself.

Sign of the cross. I stand, looking at myself in the mir-ror one more time, one last time. It's the eyes, always the eyes. There's a language in them. What do I see? Help-less. Sad. Alone. Disintegrating. Desperate. I see my great-grandfather; his eyes are mine. He was a man I never knew, but the darkness began with him, or maybe even earlier. I know his sad secrets are my own.

I put the cup to my mouth and reach for the water cup.

There's a smack and a zap. The light flickers, then off. Blackness. For a moment I believe I am already in that pre-death dream spiral I had longed for. But then the bottom of the plane drops out on me. I fly off my feet and my head strikes the ceiling. The pills scatter from my hand like a shotgun spraying pellets.

I tumble against the wall on my way to the floor and the light flickers on, but I am dizzy. I hear screams from outside the bathroom and I wonder if they are trying to get me out. But then the attendant tells everyone to remain calm. I try to stand, but I am too dizzy. I feel a warm sensation on my right cheek, and suddenly I notice drops of red on the floor in front of me. I put my hand to my head and it is immediately covered in sticky red blood.

I push against the walls beside me but only manage to move myself into a tucked position beside the toilet and the sink. There's a second zap and then the whole plane goes black. Again the bottom drops, but I remain jammed against the toilet this time.

A red light flashes above me and then it dies too. The

plane stops whining. I can feel it just gliding along through the air, being tossed up and down. There's no response. For a long time, we are like a dead body floating downriver, just gliding to nowhere. I wonder where I am for a second and I remember my angels and I wonder if they are holding up the plane. I wonder if this is how I am going to die.

Then there's another big drop. Fear takes hold of me and I scream as loud as I have ever screamed. When I finally breathe again, I choke on the pills left in my mouth and cough them out even as I try to swallow them. I hear terrified screams from the front of the plane, and I start to sob and pray again and again. I realize that the nose of the plane is angled downward, and the angle grows steeper by the second. And then it levels out, and the howl of the wind shrieks like a dying bird.

My stomach flips and spins and I black out. I awake a minute or an hour later; I do not know how much time has passed. But it is silent and black and for a moment I think this is it. Heaven is black and cold and silent; that's the opposite of hell, no? I touch the side of my face again and the blood is sticky but still moist. And then the plane drops suddenly, followed by a series of massive air bumps jolting me up and down. And then *smack*. Blackness descends.

Part II
Survive

Chapter 11

I wake. The room spins wildly, but I feel the force of gravity holding me down. I put my palm to the wall and steady myself. I breathe deeply. After a few moments, the whirling slows and only nausea remains. I gently touch my scalp with my other hand. There's a lump the size of a lime above my forehead. I rub it with my fingertips and caked blood crumbles off.

It is dark, but my eyes adjust and the airplane bathroom comes into focus. I remember where I am, but I don't know why I am here. Why was I left behind? I put one hand on the toilet and the other in the sink and push and pull and manage to lift myself up. The spinning accelerates and a slingshot of vomit launches from my mouth against the mirror.

My left hand finds the slotted door handle, and I pull it open. I lift myself up and then fall forward out the door. I hit the ground, but not too hard. There's a pillow of white powder thirty inches deep. My arms and legs scramble to find footing, and after a moment I stand up.

An icy wind rips across my face and it feels like a thousand tiny needles piercing me. I cover my eyes with my forearm until the gust dies down.

A dull gray light hovers over the world. *It must be morning,* I think. *We must have crashed. How long have I been out? Where am I?*

Above me are several mountain peaks. Behind me, a short rocky wall that rises a hundred feet or so to a plateau that sits like a bed with four mountain peaks for bedposts.

I pull out my gloves and hat from pockets and put them on, wincing at the pain in my head. I suddenly have an overwhelming urge to pee. I pull down my pants and semi-squat over the snow. I start to laugh out loud. I'm alone on top of a mountain in the middle of a fierce blizzard. Peeing!

I look around and take it all in. Where is everyone? Did they leave me behind? I try to remember the events of last night, but everything is fuzzy. I take a deep breath to try and clear my head.

I must try to find others. If I survived, then others must have as well.

I turn into the wind and hard, pellet-like snow hits my face. I can see only a few feet in front of me. I walk slowly, with my hands inside my coat for warmth. Scattered wreckage is everywhere. Twisted metal, ripped fabric, and mangled seats, and in the distance, what I believe is the main cabin.

The air stinks of jet fuel and smoke, and my nose burns from the fumes.

I move toward the cabin. The snow is thigh high and even waist deep in some places. My gloves are thin and my hands sting, so I put them in my pockets. What would I do without my hands? Note to self: Must find better gloves to survive.

Each step is hard work, pulling one leg up through several feet of snow and then lifting my foot out over the drift, praying that it lands on solid ground. The snow protects my legs from the sharp wind, but now I feel the cold moisture soaking through my jeans.

How much time do I have out here? A couple of hours? Maybe a day? I've read that when you crash into the ocean, the cold water rips the air from your lungs and your body goes into hypothermia in a matter of minutes. What I wouldn't give to be back in that cold sterile room at Life House right now.

I think of my window and my father's watch and the

endless hours I spent staring out onto the empty court-yard. I slide my hand into my pocket, expecting to cradle the watch, but it's gone. I check the other pocket too, but it's empty. I panic, padding down my entire jacket and pants pockets several times. Nothing. For a split second, I look all around, but I know it is useless. Nausea swells inside of me, like I've lost a piece of him again. My lip trembles, and a feeling of emptiness overwhelms me.

I look back toward the tail of the plane, but it has disap-peared behind a swirling veil of white. Then I look ahead toward what I thought a few minutes ago might be the main cabin of the plane, but I can't see beyond the blind-ing ice darting at my eyes. My heart sinks. I turn back and forth a few times hoping to see either tail or cabin, but they've disappeared behind the storm.

I'm lost. I'm going to die. On this godforsaken moun-tain, I'm going to die. Well, isn't that what I wanted?

There's no easy answer on my lips or in my mind.

Is it what I wanted? Is it?

Chapter 12

A lump rises in my throat. Tears well up and freeze on my face. I feel dizzy again and my legs buckle. I fall to my knees. Snow swishes around me, burying me, like a heartless killer shoveling dirt on top of a still-breathing victim. I'm alive, but as good as dead. I look up to where I believe the sun is, but all I see are patterns of gray and white dancing before my eyes.

A huge sob heaves up, and I let out a primal scream that emerges from the darkest part of my heart. It is as if some part of me has been tied up and gagged since my father died, and now it has been let loose to be heard before it dies.

"Oh God, oh God!" I hear myself holler to the sky.

A river of uncontrollable sounds follows, cascading

up through my chest and out of my mouth. My voice has no words for what is bursting forth now. It is wild and guttural. It is life sounding off against death, before death. As I kneel and gasp, inside my head I can hear that old angelic voice whispering: *Let yourself go, Jane. Let it be. This is what you've wanted for so long. Let the clean white snow wash over you. Don't fight it; let it be joyous; let it take you and bury your sad, black heart once and forever.*

A big gust of icy air slaps my face. I tuck my head to my chest to protect myself and then, as if I have become two people, I hear my own voice dancing on the wind. And then I hear it again, but my mind knows it can't be me. Distant, clear, familiar. It keeps coming, and more clearly now, as the wind momentarily dies down.

"Help! Is somebody there?"

I start to cry for a moment and then scream back, "I'm here! Help! Help me!"

"I'm down here! Down here! I'm stuck!" the voice calls back.

"Help me!" I scream again.

Then I realize that, as desperate as I am, I am not stuck. I can move; I can act. Old Doctor's voice is echoing in my head: "It is a matter of stasis, Jane. You can wither away or help yourself. That's the only path to wellness."

I slowly lift myself out of the snow and try to steady myself. My legs wobble. My face is caked with snow and dried blood and old vomit, now beginning to freeze.

"Where are you?" I shout. "Where are you?!"

"Hello!? Hello!?" the voice shouts. And then, "Down here! Down here!"

I know that voice. I know that annoying, but now so incredibly beautiful, voice. It's Paul Hart. I start moving through the deep snow. My legs pump like adrenaline-fueled pistons, slashing through the drifts with urgency and purpose. My head and heart fill with hope and my body takes flight. I feel like I'm almost running on top of the snow.

I look up and I see the sky opening up below my feet and I jam my heels hard into the snow. My feet skid and then I fall on my butt, sliding to the very edge of a crevice.

I nudge my head over the side, careful not to slip in the process. I look down, and it is black and bottomless. It must be hundreds of feet deep. My heart stops for a second, and then my stomach wrenches when I think how close I came to running right off the edge of the world.

I lean back and inhale deeply, then peer over the side again and see that Paul, a good twenty feet below me, is still strapped in his airplane seat, which is lodged into a tree that is growing out of the side of the mountain.

"Are you all right?" I shout.

He looks up at me from his perch and smiles.

"Just my fucking luck, they've sent a philosopher to save me!"

"What?" I say reflexively.

He looks down and then up at me.

"I'm in one piece, but my seat belt is jammed. I can't get out. Is it just us?" he asks.

"I don't think so," I shout. "I don't really know."

"There's a knife in my bag. Did the plane survive? Did you find any bags?"

"I saw wreckage," I shout.

I don't move. I'm just staring at his face. Then I say absurdly, "Are you cold?"

"What?" he snaps, momentarily exasperated. "Yes, I'm very cold! Listen, the knife is in my yellow backpack; do you have access to any of the luggage? Is anyone else here?"

"There are bags everywhere—I think the bay opened when we crashed," I say.

"Look for rope, too, and a sleeping bag or something to protect me if I have to spend the night here."

"Okay," I shout.

I turn to walk, but he calls out again.

"Wait, what's your name?"

"What?"

"I don't know your name," he shouts.

"Jane," I say. "Jane Solis."

Chapter 13

I inhale the frozen air and let it fill my lungs. My mind fires up and I turn from the ledge and look back across the frozen land. The wind dies down and I can see the thin strip on which the captain crashed the plane. It is a plateau a couple hundred yards wide and perhaps twice as long. It is dotted with thick evergreen trees and shrouded on all sides by mountain peaks. *It was pure dumb random luck,* I think. *We hit a tiny runway tucked on the side of a mountain. A hundred yards more in any direction and we're dead.*

Whatever footprints I made on my way to the ledge have been swept away by the wind. An impenetrable wall of snow and ice moves sideways through the air. I can see neither tail nor wreckage. I close my eyes and imagine my trek to this ledge and then my way back. I open them and step forward with an odd air of confidence.

This isn't a want. You need to save Paul. You have no choice, Jane. Just go forward.

I take my first step and then a second. Slowly, I trudge through the deep drifts of snow. Each step requires an enormous exertion of energy. I steel myself against the wind and ice, and I let my legs take over. One foot in front of the other until, after ten minutes, in the near distance, I glimpse a speck of red in a sea of white. Lettering, a number, I do not know what it is yet, but through the squall I lock my eyes onto that one spot. *It must be the body of the plane.*

With a shot of hope to charge me up, my right leg flies out of the drift and then my left. Step over step, again and again, I move through the deep snow without thinking, just staring at that bit of red.

The red gets brighter and deeper, but it isn't a number or a letter. I'm about five feet away, a couple of strides perhaps, when I see a red boot sticking straight up out of the snow. There's a leg attached. And then about two or three feet from the leg, I see the captain's head, turned on its side, detached from its body, staring at me.

I open my mouth to scream, but nothing comes out until my guts clench and I dry heave specks of dark green bile onto the snow.

There's no air in my lungs and my stomach turns again and the sound that comes out of my body is deep and soul-scraping, like a wounded animal torn in half by a trap. I look around and see luggage, clothing, debris, and what appears to be a woman with her arm draped over the snow at the near entrance of the main cabin. Her hand is still adorned with a giant ring.

"Margaret," I whisper.

It is weird and unexpected, but a lump grows in my throat. *This is so fucking random. I'm alive and Margaret's dead. Why do I deserve to live? I don't. I don't.*

I imagine Eddie, and Margaret's sisters and brothers, her mother and father, all of who are hoping right now that she'll be the lucky one. I can hear Eddie's voice as clearly as if I were still standing in line behind him: "If anyone survives, it'll be Margaret. She's a survivor." Well, I guess we all are until we're not.

And then my mother's face pops into my mind. That sad, broken face she wore for years after my father died. For a moment I try hard to remember what her face was like on that Christmas Eve before he died. We made cookies. I wonder if she remembers? I wonder if across the continent, our brains could be connecting right now. If she believes I'm a survivor.

Chapter 14

The entrance to the shell of the plane is a few yards beyond Margaret's hand. Against the hard-falling snow, it sits like a gigantic metal sculpture, unveiled only for my eyes. I move slowly and assuredly through the snow until my hands find the cold metal. I work my way around to a jagged hole once occupied by the plane's tail, entering what was formally the entire middle section of the plane. There's another gaping void on the other side where the door to the pilot's cabin used to be.

The plane must have broken into three parts: the tail, with the bathroom and me; the body, which I'm now standing in; and the pilot's cabin, wherever that may be. I walk the aisle and stop at a man who is still strapped into his seat. He is ice cold, eyes frozen open with the dull glow of death. I look and check the others quickly. The few who remain strapped into their seats are dead. The others are outside, dismembered. No movement, no life.

Then I turn to look at my row and both seats are gone, just ripped out. They were probably thrown because they appear to have been situated right where the end of the plane tore from the middle section. That's how Paul survived.

A big gust pushes through the shell and I realize how cold I am and how little shelter the cabin offers me since it's wide open on either end. I look around. Bags are everywhere. Books, toiletries, clothes. The cargo bay has been ripped open, and luggage is strewn across the snow.

Then I see the first piece of good news I've had since finding Paul. It's the green duffle bag the climbers jammed under the seats in front of us. *I'd bet my life it is full of hiking stuff.*

I try to grab its handle, but my hands are cold and getting a firm grip is difficult. Instead, I try looping my elbow around and pulling back like a mule. It won't budge and the zipper is wedged tight against the seats. I move myself to the front of the next row and sit on the floor. With my back braced against the seats, I push against the bag with my feet. It nudges forward.

I get up and go back to the other side of the seats. I look at the seat and then pull off the seat cushion, remove the life jacket, and underneath I can see the zipper of the bag. I stand on top of the bag and stamp it down as much as I can. I walk around to the back and I spend a minute blowing on my right hand and fingers until they feel warmer. I grasp the handle at the end of the bag with my right hand and wrap my left around for support. I yank, and it moves, but only an inch. I try again by leveraging my feet against the seats in front of me and push with my legs while pulling with my arms. Nothing.

I laugh for a second. *You have to laugh,* I tell myself.

I stand up and assess. I have to get inside this damn bag. I kneel and bite down hard on the zipper tag, niggling my teeth against the little hole on the end. Then, like a dog, I pull the zipper as hard as I can with my teeth. For a moment I feel no movement, no give, but then the zipper loosens and gives an inch. I start yanking and yanking against the opening until *zip!* It moves six inches, then a foot. I grab the two ends with my hands and pull it open as wide as I can.

I reach in. Bingo. I pull out a pair of good gloves and a snow mask and put them on. Suddenly, I'm feeling a little buoyancy.

I take out several pairs of long underwear and wool socks and place them on the seat. I slip off my boots and peel off my snow-wet jeans. The cold wind stings my bare legs, which are blotchy and red. I pull on the first pair of long underwear, then the socks and a baggy pair of snow pants. I tuck a second pair of long johns and a dry pair of jeans for Paul underneath my coat.

I pull out a wind shell that I quickly put on.

Underneath, I find a sweater and a stash of energy bars. I tuck them down my shirt and zip up the shell.

There's undoubtedly more stuff in the rest of the plane.

I walk down the aisle opening the overhead luggage bins. I pull down what I assume is a sleeping bag brought by one of the climbers. I slide my arm under the bungee cords wrapped around the bag and strap it across my back like a makeshift knapsack. I open the next overhead bin. I leap out of the way as luggage falls out. I start popping open the bags one by one. Hats, gloves. Pants. Sweaters. Wool socks! I grab three pairs and I stuff the extra gloves and hat into the pockets of my shell. I pull out a scarf and wrap it around my neck. I find a bag of chips I pocket for later.

Halfway down the aisle, I find another one of the climber's bags and I pull it down. It's stuffed with ropes and all sorts of other, unrecognizable gear. I loop a coil of rope around my shoulder. I look for a knife or any other sharp objects, but there's nothing.

The yellow bag, I think. *Find the yellow bag.*

Chapter 15

I walk out of the main cabin and look at the graveyard of luggage strewn across the snow. All this stuff must have been in the cargo belly of the plane, which tore open like a tin can on landing.

I look for yellow rather than the shape of the backpack. Every color in the rainbow pokes up bright and clear against the canvas of white. Red sweaters, brown shoes, toothbrushes and makeup, tan pants and striped shirts. Black bags. Red bags. Pink. Orange. White. And about twenty feet from the far end of the cabin sits a neon yellow backpack.

I push through deep drifts, my right hand grazing the cold metal of the main cabin for balance. When I reach the end, I turn left and walk twenty feet out, wading through a pile of unopened bags until I reach what I really hope is Paul's backpack. I fish around inside the main pocket of his bag until I locate his knife. I pull it out. The blade is sharp and thick, jagged at the tip. A day ago, had I stumbled upon this in Life House, I wouldn't have thought twice about using it on myself. Now using it for any purpose other than to save Paul is inconceivable. I unzip my jacket and tuck the knife in the side pocket reserved for wallets and keys.

I sling Paul's bag over my shoulder, next to the sleeping bag. My burden is bulky and the weight is top-heavy and uneven, making it difficult to walk. A few steps are all it takes for me to know that carrying it to the ledge will be too time-consuming. I take it off and shove it under the roof of the main cabin to protect it from the snow. I trudge back along the outside of the main cabin, using my hand for balance, and then out toward the ledge, with the rope over my shoulder and Paul's clothes under my jacket. I pat my side pocket several times to make sure Paul's knife is still there.

I get back to the ledge and look over at Paul. I call to him, but he doesn't hear me. The wind has picked up and it makes it difficult to hear anything.

I scream, "Paul," as loud as I can, and then I kick some snow and he looks up.

"Hey," he says.

We stare at each other for a brief moment. Even from this distance, or maybe because of it, there's a lot in his eyes: fear, death, and a kind of desperate loneliness I understand but could never explain in words.

I look down and really study Paul's predicament for the first time. He is sitting twenty feet below the ledge, wedged between a tree and the slope of the mountain. It is closer to a cliff than a mountain slope. He is still fastened into his seat by his seat belt, which is jammed. If he were to somehow cut away the belt, I don't see any conceivable way he could exit his seat without causing the whole thing to tumble to the valley floor. Even if he were to hang onto a tree and climb to the top, he'd still be ten feet from the ledge. With great weather and the right equipment, I suppose it could be climbed. But we're missing both. I look to the sky and then back down at Paul.

"What should I do?" I ask.

"Tie the rope around the knife and lower it to me. Be very careful; it's my life on the line." He laughs. Everything is still a joke to him. In the hospital, I never liked his type.

The snow starts to fall again, not too hard, but it is being blown sideways by the wind, making it more difficult to wrap the rope around the knife. Instead, I make a loop of the rope and pull it against the tip of the blade. I jiggle the tip back and forth until it slices through the rope. Then I wrap the rope around the handle and tie a knot and double it—it's the only knot I know how to make.

I slowly feed the rope over the edge and gently drop the blade down to Paul. He reaches out and pulls in the rope and the blade and wraps the rope around his forearm. One of his hands must be cold because he's using his mouth to undo the knot.

"Don't cut yourself," I shout.

"That's a good sign when the philosopher jokes," he shouts. "Means she isn't scared shitless." He pauses for a second and then looks up at me with a smile. "I'm glad one of us isn't."

He laughs to himself while perched precariously above death. Somehow I find it inspiring. I clench my fist and kneel down, nervously watching Paul maneuver in his seat.

He frees the knife by remaking the loop and holding it in one hand and pulling the knife out with his mouth. He looks up at me with the blade tight between his teeth like a pirate.

He grabs the knife with his right hand and then places it inside his jacket. He examines the seat and the tree, and I watch his eyes, trying to discern what is plaguing him, what it is he can possibly do to get out of the seat and then up the cliff.

The problem, from my viewpoint, becomes increasingly clear. The seat belt is hooked around a large branch. When cut, it will release the full weight of the seat and Paul. Another branch may hold them both up, but odds suggest he would be free-falling to his death.

"You can't cut it," I shout, fearing he hasn't figured that out.

"I know, but I have to."

Dusk is blooming above us, and because we are in a valley and the light is diminished, we should be in total darkness in less than an hour. *Then what?*

"Tie the rope around your waist. Then cut the belt. I'll secure myself here and then we'll walk you up." That's me calling down. I'm not sure where the idea comes from—or my bravado and confidence.

He watches me for a moment and makes a decision.

"Find a tree to brace yourself against!" he calls up.

I scan the area around me and choose a pine fairly close to the edge.

Paul moves the rope around his torso with one hand, and it takes longer than you might expect. He fastens a big knot he fits tightly under his armpits. He calls up to me, "Hey, I'm gonna cut this; are you ready?"

"No! Wait!"

I tie the rope around my waist and walk back maybe ten feet from the edge and crawl around a small tree whose branches sprout out a few feet above the snow. I'm careful to keep the rope free of branches that could cause fraying or a cut, but I make certain it's wrapped well around the tree. I only wish I had enough rope to go around twice. Then I get to my feet and walk to the edge, pulling the rope behind me. I hold up my thumb. He nods and then starts sawing the belt.

It starts to fray immediately, and the shoulder strap snaps free. The seat totters and then dangles in mid-air around Paul's waist. He is jammed on a branch and lets out a blood-shocking scream. It is the sound of agony itself. He slams the knife down toward his side. Then, snap! The whole seat falls and I am lifted into the air with one sudden jerk of the rope. My face and body hit the snow hard and I am dragged about five feet into the trunk of the tree. The impact is painful. I can feel where I'm going to bruise on my shoulder.

"Paul," I shout. "Paul!"

I adjust my body and straddle the base of the tree, hooking my legs around it, and hold on for my life.

"Paul! Can you hear me?" There's no answer, but his weight is still pulling against the tree.

"Paul!"

Nothing. Then suddenly the rope goes slack, and there's no longer any pressure on the line. I scream.

"Paul!"

"You need to do as I say," he calls back. "On the count of three, can you walk away from this cliff?"

I am flooded with relief.

"Yes, but count to ten; I'm kind of tangled here," I shout.

"Just say when, okay? But try to hurry."

I crawl back under the tree and free myself. The rope feels slack. I walk back to the edge and peer over. Paul is now standing in the tree and has one hand on a nub of rock. He's planning on climbing up the wall. My walking is supposed to assist him.

"What if you fall?" I call down.

He looks up and smiles.

"It'll be romantic, Jane. We'll die together, like Romeo and Juliet."

I take a big gulp of air and breathe out. *What an ass.*

"Nothing personal, but I don't want to die with you, Paul."

"That's extra incentive for you, then. Don't slip."

I make sure the knot around my waist is tight.

"Hold on a second," I call. "I have an idea."

I scurry back to the tree and crawl under and around again, creating a primitive pulley. Instead of walking away from him, I pull in all the slack, and then walk sideways, parallel to the ledge.

"Go!" I shout.

With his weight displaced against the tree, I use my lateral force to help move his weight up the mountain. I can't see him, but every time I step into fresh powder, I can sense his weight moving up the mountain.

Come on, Jane, I think. I leverage all of my one hundred and eighteen pounds into each step. Then I hear myself let out a grunt that turns into a scream, from deep inside that I didn't know was there. It's primal, like life itself announcing its return to my body. *Pull, Jane, pull.*

My feet lift out of the powder with an unbelievable force, and step after step, I feel a sense of euphoria taking over my body. Then the weight pulling against me disappears, sending my body flying forward into the snow.

I sit up and turn around, brushing snow from my face. For a second I see nothing but white. A hollow feeling fills my gut. I look to the ledge and then back over the landscape, which is flat and empty. Then, like an animal waking up after a long night hidden beneath the snow for warmth, Paul Hart pops up in my line of vision. Where did he come from? His chest heaves up and down. His face is bright red and his broad grin tells me he's okay. I start to cry as I walk over to him, I can't help it. He is still kneeling down. He looks up at me; his smile just gets bigger. He falls onto his back and lets out a big laugh.

"Jane Solis," he shouts, still flat on his back, "you pull like a donkey."

Like I said, what an ass.

Chapter 16

With some effort, Paul lifts himself into a sitting position and then stands. He looks around, surveying the area.

"Which way?" he says, still breathing heavily. "To the plane, I mean?"

No hello or "thank you for saving my life." Just "which way?" I chalk it up to his nearly dying, the thin air, and general guy-ness.

I pull out a pair of gloves and a hat and hand them to him.

"Here."

He nods and pulls back his hoodie to put the hat on, and then the gloves, but doesn't say thanks for those either. *Really?*

I point at my footprints, which are fading quickly but still visible.

"It's that way. Follow my tracks."

"Right?" He looks at me for confirmation. "Come on."

He turns and marches toward the cabin. The wind whips with a new ferocity, and the air is so cold it makes it hard to breathe. Paul walks in front, shielding me a bit from the wind with his large frame, but my teeth chatter. My throat is raw and parched and my head aches, and I realize for the first time how incredibly thirsty I am. I need water. I drop down to my knees and grab a handful of snow and start eating it. Paul turns around to see why I've stopped and reaches out to swat the snow out of my hand.

"Don't eat the snow!" he shouts.

"Why?"

"Just don't do it," he says harshly. "It can kill you."

I look directly at him for the first time. His blue eyes are bloodshot, watery, and distant. I realize I don't know who Paul is. He could be a killer or a rapist or bonkers. I laugh a little at that last one. *Maybe he's crazier than me.* I look down, trying not to get emotional or show any weakness. *Never show any sign of weakness with a psycho; they get off on it.*

"Sorry," I say.

"Stay close behind me," he commands.

He turns and trudges into the wind with his forearm covering his face. The snow has eased up a little, but the temperature has dropped and the wind is still fierce.

My nose hairs and snot freeze, and it is hard to keep my eyes open, even with a mask on. I don't know how he does it, but Paul soldiers on at a strong clip as if he were walking through a puddle on a spring day. No matter the force of the wind, he keeps a steady pace, face forward.

As we approach the plane, he stops and stares at the captain's head.

"It's the captain," I whisper, thinking he is in shock like I was when I first saw it, but then he turns to me with a weird grin on his face.

"Fuck," he says, with a nervous laugh. "That's some bad karma. Maybe if the dude had his head in the game, we wouldn't have crashed."

What a dick, I think.

I turn away and kneel down for a second, pretending to look for something while I try to catch my breath. When I look up, Paul's already moved on toward the captain's leg, which is sticking out of the snow. I want to run up and grab his shoulders, turn him around, and slap him across the face. Remind him that these are human beings, that life is sacred even if it's mostly just a pile of shit.

But I know it's a waste. He'll laugh in my face. This is why great comedians end up on drugs or killing themselves, according to BS. If everything in life's a joke, then nothing has any meaning. If there's no meaning, why live? You get the logic.

I watch Paul from a safe distance. He's digging the snow around the leg and the body. After a few minutes, he unearths the headless body. He opens the captain's jacket and sticks his hands in the inside pocket, pulling out a pack of cigarettes, which he stuffs in his own jacket, and then he pulls out the captain's aviator sunglasses and holds them up like he's found buried treasure. He puts them on and turns to me, pointing to his new shades with a "what do ya think?" look on his face.

I'm disgusted, but I hold my tongue. I have to be with Paul until we get ourselves out of here. I need him. I can't afford to piss him off.

"No lighter. We need a damn lighter."

He pushes on toward the carcass of the plane and we enter from the far side. I stand and watch Paul as he grabs his yellow backpack. I was right: this is his bag. He opens the bag and digs into it, pulling out a little black notebook. He pauses and stares at it for a moment and then tucks it into the lining of his jacket and slings the backpack onto his back.

"I forgot about this," he says, pointing to his backpack. "I've got wet matches in here. We'll be good."

He looks around and takes in what lies before him. The open-ended cabin, the swirling wind. There's no protection here. He looks up to the sky.

"It's getting dark—is this it?" he says. "We'll fucking freeze to death here."

"No," I say. "The tail, it has the bathroom. There's a door."

"Which way?"

I point toward the direction of the tail. He walks past me without so much as *thanks* or an *excuse me* or *good work*. *Despise* doesn't quite describe the deep, roiling hatred that I am developing for Paul Hart.

On his way out of the cabin, he spots Margaret and he holds up her hand, pointing to the ring. "That's a whopper!"

A rage explodes inside of me and I'm unable to hold back.

"Shut up," I shout. "They're dead. She's dead. People are waiting for her."

Paul stops for a moment.

"What?"

"They're human beings," I shout. "Her name is Margaret!"

Paul stands there frozen in the snow, just staring at me and apparently bewildered by my rage.

"They're not garbage to be picked over and laughed at." I sound defensive, which is ridiculous.

Paul stands motionless for a moment and then looks down at Margaret and then, lifting his sunglasses, at me again. His gaze is blank.

"Dead is dead. She's not here anymore." I try again.

He looks up, like he's acknowledging heaven, though I can't imagine for a second that he gives any currency to that belief system. I just stare at him as tears well up in my eyes. I feel a sadness I can't place. I can't move or speak, and my bones feel like they are crumbling. I start to shake uncontrollably and my mouth opens but nothing comes. Warm tears flow and freeze on my face. I'm having trouble breathing and then my head starts to spin. The world turns upside down, and for a split second I feel like I'm falling.

Paul springs toward me and puts his arms around me, keeping me up. He holds me very tight, like my father did when I was a little girl.

"Hold on, Solis. Steady."

I can't believe this is same guy who joked about the captain's head.

My body continues to shake uncontrollably. He squeezes

me tighter and tighter, constantly whispering, "Breathe . . . breathe . . . breathe," until I gain control.

And then something unexpected happens. I hear myself speak, and not sarcastically or vaguely, or with anger or rage, but with honesty.

"I should be the dead one, not Margaret," I say, pointing to her body.

"Did you know her?" he asks.

"Not exactly," I say. "I mean, a little. She had a whole life; she was a newlywed and she had Eddie at home who loved her more than life itself."

"Sometimes luck makes you feel guilty," Paul says softly. "You can't beat yourself up for still being here."

He doesn't even know what I'm talking about, but he has said the right thing. All that life Margaret had to look forward to, all that life I was trying to wreck and throw away. None of it matters. I was the lucky one. She wasn't. And now I feel guilty about it. The same way I felt guilty about living and my father dying. Why should we carry on when the people we love are dead?

"Doesn't anything matter?" I say as a few tears roll down my cheek.

I look up and see his eyes and I swear I see tears building. He looks down at me curiously and then drops his sunglasses back down.

"Are you okay?" he says again, wanting to move on.

"I should be dead."

"I understand."

"No you don't. I tried to kill myself last night, in the bathroom, before the plane crashed. That's why I survived. It's fucked up. I'm so fucked up."

I don't know why I chose to tell him at this moment, in a frozen graveyard of bodies, or why my normally impenetrable steel vault is suddenly wide open for him to see into, but there it is.

"What do you mean?" he says. I can't see his eyes, but his mouth is twisted with anguish and his upper lip trembles. I think he's trying to say something—anything—to be helpful, but he can't find the words. I finally blurt out a river of thoughts.

"I started to take pills in the bathroom, then the plane crashed, and I woke up alive. I should be dead, but I'm not. She should be alive, but isn't."

Paul stands there like a statue, looking at me and through me, trying to process his thoughts as quickly as he can. I can imagine some of those thoughts: *Holy shit, I'm on a mountain with a freakazoid; Hide the knife, she could kill us both; Don't let her at the minibar, if I can find it.*

But he only says, "If you weren't lucky, I'd be dead. It's not just about you."

His mouth relaxes and a big smile crosses his face, like he's proud that he just put together a little philosophical escape hatch for me.

"Thanks," I mutter.

He wraps his arms around me one more time and rubs my back. His arms make me feel warm and remind me of how cold I am.

"I'm so cold," I say, sniffling. "You must be frozen."

"I am," he says.

"This way," I say. I grab his hand and pull. We walk silently together to the tail of the plane.

Chapter 17

By the time we cross the short stretch to the tail, it is nearly dark. We open the door and slide in. It's tight, but we manage to stand side by side, though we are forced to lean against the wall to accommodate the tilt.

Paul looks around for a second.

"This is good."

I reach into my jacket and hand him an energy bar and some chips. He just looks at it, sheepishly.

"My hands are too numb. I can't open it."

I take off my mittens and put one end of the bar into my mouth and tear the packaging open. I hand it back to Paul. He holds it in his gloves and bites half off and hands me the rest. It's semi-frozen, and we have a tough time chewing.

Paul points to the chips and I rip them open. We both grab a handful and shovel them into our mouths. I immediately realize this is a mistake and Paul does too. We look at each other trying to chew up the semi-frozen, taffy-like energy bar and the greasy chips and start to laugh. We crunch and chew and crunch, but the giant wads in our mouths never get smaller. Paul starts to make his chewing exaggerated and then he tries to speak, which is apparently impossible with potato chips and energy bar in your mouth.

"Wwwwtter."

"What?"

He pantomimes drinking and I shake my head.

"Noooothing?" he says.

I shake my head again. I look at him closely for the first time as my eyes adjust to the light. His entire body is shaking uncontrollably. I reach up and take his sunglasses off and touch his face. For the first time, I notice how little he's wearing. If he didn't have his jacket on, he would be dead. But it isn't a thick jacket, though that can be deceiving.

But he is wearing jeans and, from what I can tell, only a flannel shirt underneath the jacket.

"You're freezing. My God."

I quickly pull out the clothes I had jammed under my jacket and hand them to him.

He looks at his boots and then to me.

"Can you unlace them for me?"

I take off my gloves and tug on the laces and loosen up the knots. Then I pull the boot apart the best I can.

"Pull with your leg and I'll hold," I say.

There's some resistance, but eventually his foot slides out. I unlace the next one and it slides off too.

"The socks too."

I slowly peel off his socks, which causes a few yelps from Paul.

"Fuck, that burns," he says through gritted teeth.

"Sorry," I say. "I'm trying to be careful."

Every part of his body is frozen red, and when I touch him, little white spots appear on his skin. His clothing is damp from the snow. The cliff protected him from the worst of the storm, especially the wind, but hanging out there for hours left him exposed.

"My pants, please," he says, still trying to flex his hands.

I look up at him. His eyes are soft, sky blue. I nod, like it doesn't bother me in the least. I've never taken a guy's pants off before, and this certainly isn't how I expected it would go down: on top of mountain, in the bathroom of a crashed plane, in the middle of a blizzard.

I put my hands on his jeans. There's a belt that I loosen

and then pull off. I unbutton the fly and unzip. I put my fingers around his waist and grip both sides. I turn my head to the side and yank down as hard as I can. He lifts one leg and I pull the pant leg over his foot, then the next.

"And these—they're soaked," he says, feeling the back of his briefs.

My eyebrows go up instinctually and I say, "Really?"

He puts his hands out in front of me and for the first time I see how red and bruised they are.

"Okay, sorry. I'm gonna close my eyes."

He smiles and shakes his head. "Sorry. I apologize for the weirdness."

I close my eyes and slide my hand beneath the band at his waist and slowly pull them down as he steps out. I grab the long johns and open them up so he can step in them, which he does. I stand up and pull them over his crotch. I sneak a peek and feel a flush spread across my face. I never look up, afraid he'll see me blushing.

I grab the dry jeans and repeat the whole process in reverse. When I'm done, I put dry wool socks on both of us.

I watch Paul pull down the bottom of his jeans over his socks with clumsy, swollen hands. I have an impulse to touch them, which is unexpected because they look gross. I don't act on it. Instead, I look up into his eyes, and he's staring down at me.

"Hey," I say.

"Thank you," he says. "We should sleep together."

"Excuse me?"

"Sorry, in the sleeping bag, I mean. This is decent shelter, but our warmth is our greatest asset; we'll maximize it in the bag. We'll figure something else out when it's light again."

"Right," I say nonchalantly. Inside, I'm shouting, *Holy shit, holy shit.*

Then I add, "Yeah, makes total sense."

We both step into the bag, and I slowly zip it up. It is really snug, and the front of his body presses against my back. We fit like crescent moons lying side by side. His body, despite being dressed in dry clothes, emits a coldness I can only imagine is painful to bear. His hands are right in front of me to study. His right hand is red and cold, but his left is bruised and cut. They both look angry and swollen. Then, as though he can see me staring at them, he speaks: "I'm going to put my hands on you, okay? I need the warmth."

Slowly his hands move under my jacket and my sweater, his long arms circling me, and then he tucks his hands under my arms. Blood rushes to my cheeks and my stomach drops with unexpected excitement. I've never been touched like this before, and though it's probably just platonic, I feel a pulse of electricity shoot through my body.

"Is that too awful?" he asks. "I'm sorry."

"It's okay," I say. But his body heat is good, much better than being in the bag alone. Instinctively, I cross my arms and place my hands over his. He grunts from the pain.

"Your hands aren't as soft as I remember," he whispers in my ear.

I smile, thinking of our first conversation.

"I can't believe we're here," I say.

"I can't believe you're sleeping with me after one day."

"Yeah, but I can't believe you let me know your little secret," I say.

"What secret is that, my philosopher friend?"

"You make jokes when you're nervous, so I guess sharing a sleeping bag with me makes you nervous?"

I know he's smiling—I can feel it in my heart. He says nothing for a long time. We just lie there on our sides, listening to the wind and our breathing. Our feet press against the wall beside the toilet and our heads lie softly on our coats.

"Thank you," he whispers.

"I'm not a philosopher," I whisper back. "I mean, I'm not a philosophy major. I lied before, so you can stop calling me that. Please."

There's a pause in the darkness. I don't know where all the courage is coming from, but I do know I feel an uncontrollable urge not to lie. Not to lie going forward, not to lie period.

"Right," he says. And then he adds an aside a few moments later: "But I can tell you think too much. Sometimes doing is better than thinking, you know?"

"Not really," I say.

Suddenly, he kisses the top of my head, in a brotherly way, nothing further.

"See, I wanted to do that, but I was thinking about it too much."

"Clever," I say.

"Night," he whispers.

I sit for a moment in the dark, thinking about the day. It's been endless and utterly exhausting—like a lifetime lived in twenty-four hours. I can hear a soft snore coming from Paul. I wonder what tomorrow will bring.

Chapter 18

I wake. Light splinters in from under the door. Paul's arms are draped around me: his right arm snakes around my body, and his left circles above and around, cupping my waist, his hand gripping my side just above the hip bone.

I've read about the wilderness and I know that you can experience hallucinations in extreme cold. Because there's a twenty-ish guy spooning me, I question whether this is indeed a hallucination. Am I losing my mind? I consider the possibility that I am actually dead and that this is the beginning of an unexpected afterlife. Could I have conjured up a more conventional scenario than to wake up in the arms of a beautiful boy?

I don't want to move, for fear of waking him. I listen to his breathing, which is full and deep. His breath is warm on my neck. Maybe somebody will come today and find us and it will all be over. I wish I had a close friend I could tell. There's nobody at the institution but the Old Doctor. He'd love it. I can imagine him saying, "Jane, don't you see now? You were alive up there, face-to-face with death. Things happen when you're alive in the world."

"Are you awake?" Paul's voice is deep and rusty.

"Yes, why?"

"You were talking to yourself. I thought maybe you were dreaming." He shifts around a bit, moving his right arm up to stretch it.

"What was I saying?" I ask.

"You don't want to know."

Oh my God.

"Tell me, please," I say.

"I'm kidding."

Thank you, God.

"My hands feel better," he remarks as he flexes his bruised left fingers. "But my head is killing me.

"Mine hurts too," I say.

"We're dehydrated. A headache is the first sign from the body. We need to find water."

That's true, no doubt, but what I'm thinking is I really have to pee badly. The bizarre nature of this situation dawns on me. I'm sharing a bathroom, literally, with a guy I met, in real time, maybe three hundred words ago. Sure, we survived an airplane crash together and I saved his life and I guess we have slept together, which may have created a bond so profound it will transcend time, but the thought of peeing in front of him still feels way out of the question.

"I hate to break this up," he whispers.

"Why are you whispering?"

"What do you mean?" he says.

"You're whispering and we're alone in the middle of nowhere, in a bathroom."

"Right," he agrees, and then shouts loudly: "Nobody can hear us, can they?"

Not a hallucination: he's just as annoying now as he was when I first met him. But I can't help finding some of his antics charming.

He reaches over and pulls the zipper down on the sleeping bag.

"We need to do some investigating. And I actually need to use the toilet," he confides.

"Me too. The bathroom."

We both stand, he hunched over and me leaning against the sink, and look at each other for a minute.

"I'm not peeing in front of you," I say.

"Right."

He steps into his boots and laces them up. He pulls the door open and looks back out at me. "Don't take too long; it's freezing out here."

He steps out into the light and pulls the door shut. I know he can still hear me and hearing is almost worse than seeing. Either way I have stage fright, so to speak.

"Start singing," I shout.

"What?"

"I said start singing so you can't hear me pee."

"That's ridiculous."

"Start singing or I won't pee." I start kicking the door with my foot. "And I won't let you in."

He clears his throat and then breaks into song. *"Every cheap hood strikes a bargain with the world, ends up making love to a sofa or girl . . . Death or glory, just another story."*

I immediately let go, which is the most glorious sense of relief I've ever felt in my life. When I'm done, I move my foot and stand up and adjust. Then I pull the door slightly in to indicate I'm finished. Paul quickly jumps in and pushes the door shut. We are standing face-to-face. The top of my head only reaches his chin, which is black and stubbly.

I look up into his blue eyes.

"It's very cold," he says.

"I wasn't aware."

"Sarcastic, are you?"

"Yes."

"Well, it isn't just cold. It's bitter cold. It's negative cold."

"That means exactly nothing to me," I say.

"Do you really want to know?"

"Yes, I do."

"Well," he mumbled. "My pee—it froze as it hit the snow. It has to be very, you know, cold. It must have dropped forty or fifty degrees last night." He paused. "And the wind is kicking powder and ice around; feels like flying needles on your face."

"Someone will find us soon, don't you think?"

"I wouldn't count on it."

"But they always find people when they crash. They must know we've crashed."

"Not in a blizzard and on a mountain in the Bob Marshall Wilderness," he says. "Even if they knew where we were, it could take days or weeks to get climbers up here . . . With this amount of snow, we might not be found for weeks, maybe months."

"Bob what?"

"Bob Marshall Wilderness. There are no roads. It's two hundred and fifty miles of roadless mountains, and I think we've landed somewhere in it."

"How will we get out?"

"I'm not sure, but down here they'll never find us," he says gravely.

"If you're trying to scare me, you'll have to do better than that," I say, remembering all the cuts and blood and pain that landed me at Life House in the first place. Slowly watching yourself die and being unable to respond sounds wildly familiar to me. In fact, I think freezing to death sounds pretty straightforward.

"Do you know what happens when you die of dehydration?"

"I think so." Now he's starting to scare me because I am so thirsty, my saliva is sticking to my tongue and cheeks like paste.

"Well, here's the thing: you can eat the snow and freeze to death, or we can stay here and die of dehydration."

"Is there a third option?"

"The plane. We have to skin it clean of every drop of water and every morsel of food and every piece of equipment we can find in it."

"And after that?"

"We'll decide when the time comes."

Chapter 19

Bounty isn't exactly the word I'd use to describe what we found rummaging through the luggage (me) and bodies (Paul) left on the plane. We found four candy bars, a pack of gum (the old-fashioned sugary kind), cough syrup, sleeping pills (Paul pocketed those), Tylenol, a lighter, some plastic garbage bags from the snack service (for keeping stuff dry), two empty plastic soda bottles (Paul says we'll fill them with snow and our bodies will melt them into water over time), a first aid kit, lots of non-working cell phones, one Sawtooth Mountain coffee mug, a camping lantern, a pair of sunglasses for me. And a second sleeping bag, which I immediately recognize as the end of my very short-lived physical experience with the opposite sex.

I follow him back to the tail of the plane, the wind at our backs now, so we make good time. We stop outside. For the first time, the sky is clear enough to see the outside of our shelter. The tail of the plane remains intact. The little wing on the right side of the tail is jammed into the snow, and the left wing sticks out at a forty-five-degree angle. The rudder streaks toward the sky and looms tall over the ledge, like the top of a broken cross marking a wintry grave.

I look at the bathroom door—it's tilted sideways in the middle of the exposed circle that once seamlessly attached to the main cabin. The metal surrounding it is distressed; I imagine it having a voice and screaming from the pain of being ruthlessly torn from its body. Crooked and slightly indented at the middle, the door represents the flimsy line of protection between the wilderness and us.

Paul pushes open the bathroom door and starts arranging all the stuff we found inside. I walk behind the tail of the plane and am hit by a toxic wall of spilled jet fuel. The snow is saturated with a bluish-green hue that streaks back from behind the plane. The winds, I think, must have pushed the fumes away from our cabin. I quickly cover my mouth and nose, but the stench is strong, and the combination of hunger and dehydration and the fumes overwhelms me. I begin to wobble, and Paul's hand suddenly grabs my forearm.

"Whoa—you can't inhale that stuff at all. It'll kill you."

"Sorry," I mumble.

"That's one of the reasons we can't stay here. If the winds shift, we'll be inhaling jet fuel all day and night."

I nod, but I'm too weak to process the phrase "can't stay here." It rings in my mind, but I can't quite bring myself to confront it or Paul.

Paul walks me back and opens the door.

"You first," he says.

I step in, and Paul has organized things like a little nest for us. It makes my heart warm. He climbs in behind me, and it is snugger than before. He's so big and the tail so tilted and cramped that all we can do is lean against the wall together, in a semi-lying-standing position.

We get settled in our bag and then Paul hands me the coffee mug filled with snow. We look at the rest of our loot, which I've laid out on the floor: basically candy bars, which I could eat by myself for one lunch, but that's all we have and we'll have to make it last.

"Hold up the mug," he says.

He takes his tiny lantern, breaks the glass around the flame and lights it. It provides almost no heat, but Paul places the cup directly onto the flame and melts the snow.

"Why don't we just eat the snow?"

"Like I said before, you'll die. We're already at risk for hypothermia. Eating snow will drop your body temperature even more. Eventually, we will use our bodies to melt the snow in these soda bottles, but we need water now. That's more important than food by a long shot."

We wait silently for a long time as snow turns to slush and slush to water. I sip the warm water as it crests to the top. It is heaven in the form of water. I've never tasted anything as sweet in my life. I look at Paul as he takes his first sip and I can tell he's thinking the same thing I am, which is that I've never been truly thirsty before. I've never, by turn, ever appreciated how wonderful water is. I laugh, thinking there were days in the institution when I was so depressed that the thought of drinking or eating something depressed me more. That seems unimaginable to me now.

We wait for more to melt. It is agonizingly slow. But each warm mouthful feels like a cup of heaven in your mouth and throat. We look at each other, understanding that each sip is sacred, not to be taken for granted.

Then the light flickers for a few minutes and it dies. *Fuck* is all I can think. Paul's face looks grave.

"How long?" I say, my eyes cast downward on our last cup of water.

"Who knows?"

"Best guess?"

"After the weather breaks, and not before then. I'd bet two to three weeks minimum."

I think of all the news stories about crashed planes and can't help but wonder about the black box and GPS.

"Shouldn't they be able to find us with some kind of scanner or something?"

"Like on TV? It doesn't work that way. We are in the mountains and it's snowing. There's probably three hundred miles between us and what we'd call civilization."

"But still," I respond. "They can find anything."

"Last year, a twin engine crashed somewhere I reckon was not far from here with four passengers. In the summer. It took them almost a month to find the plane. I mean, they can probably say it's around here, but 'around here' is under a blanket of snow, in fields of evergreens, and perched one hundred feet below the top of a remote mountain."

After his speech, we sit in silence. I don't know what to say or think. I want to believe that we will just be saved, but then I hear Paul's voice and it sounds so clear and rational. He would know, right?

"And the people?" I ask.

"Pancaked on impact," he says wryly. "We got a leg up

on them there."

Two weeks on four candy bars and a cup of melted water as long as the butane in the lantern lasts. I calculate and don't like the odds.

"Can we make it?"

"Possibly, possibly not. Two weeks is a long time."

"We're a little protected here, but we're too hidden; is that what you're thinking? That this feels safe, but wouldn't we be better off up there?" I ask, gesturing up the mountain.

"Yes, you're right. But getting up there will be tough. Do you think you're up for it? It's a nasty climb."

"I want to live," I say weirdly. Oh my God, I must seem like a total freak to him. I look away and around our little room. He must sense my awkwardness because he squeezes my arm in friend-like way.

"I can see that."

I nod, having been more honest with Paul than perhaps any person on earth. I think back on all my sessions with the Old Doctor, and I know I never told him that I out and out wanted to hit the switch. When I tried to do it before coming to the institution, I really wanted to succeed. I can see myself for a second, standing in the bathroom two nights ago, with destiny in my palm. I would never have hoped for a plane crash, and it saddens me more that others died, but I am so grateful for the second chance.

"I'm sorry," he says.

"About?"

"The head—you know, the jokes. It wasn't funny. I didn't think it was; I just didn't know what else to do. I say stupid things when I'm nervous."

I rub one of his hands and then just hold it. In my heart, I believe this is the real Paul. Underneath those man-made veneers is a boy with a big heart who is afraid to be who he is. *But why?* I wonder. *This is going to be okay, I think. Everything is going to be okay.*

Chapter 20

I wake from a deep, dreamless sleep. I am tired but alert and rejuvenated. "The sleep of the just," my grandfather used to say to me. At home, I was known for my sleeping prowess, able to leap past a whole day in a single nap. But I never felt well rested, just depressed and sluggish and empty.

There is light poking through a crack in the door. My body is exhausted, but the little speckle of light pulls at me. I reach back to touch Paul, but I realize he is not there. For a moment I panic, and the thought that he has abandoned me makes my heart rate speed up. I quickly twist and turn around our tiny compartment. It takes me all of one-point-three seconds to survey the airplane bathroom—aka our survival bunker: toilet, check; sink, check; supplies, check; Paul, no check.

Then I see a note propped up against a wool hat carefully positioned between the back wall and the latrine. The bottom of the note is slotted into the folded cuff of the hat so it acts like an old-fashioned letter stand. Written in black ink and typical male chicken scratch, the note is on a little piece of torn paper. The stock of the paper is heavy and lightly textured, like from a diary or an expensive, old-fashioned notebook.

I pick it up and read.

Solis—Off to survey—Stay put—will come back 4 u. P

Beneath the hat, I spy a corner of the little black book Paul had tucked into the lining of his jacket during yesterday's scavenger hunt. A flicker of memory zips through my brain and I recall the slightly pained look on his face as he stared at it momentarily. I pick it up, and even though every instinct in my body tells me not to open it, not to pry, not to violate his privacy or something sacred to him . . . I succumb. He looked so pained by it, I rationalize, perhaps I could help him. I am, I tell myself, experienced in the art of psychology. Just a peek inside, distill a little info, and then a diagnosis, perhaps followed by a cure? *Anyway, I should know more about him,* I reason. *He could be anyone.*

I feel the cover with my hand first. The black leather is smooth and worn. I open it up and look inside. There's a name carved into the inside of the leather cover, but it's been scratched out. I can still make it out: *Will Hart. For Paul* is etched in blue ink below.

Lying inside is a photo of Paul and, I assume, Will. They look like twins, but Will is obviously Paul's senior by a year or so. The picture was taken from inside a hospital room and Will is in a blue hospital gown. Paul's face is long and sad and beaten, but there's stoicism there as well. I turn it over, and on the upper-right-hand corner of the photo, *Will's eighteenth birthday* is written.

All the pages in the diary are blank and pressed in a way that suggests the pages have never been turned. I fan through trying to find any signs of writing, but there's nothing.

In the back, I find a letter written on what my grandfather would have called onionskin paper. It is thin and practically see-through. Back in the day before email and texting, people used this stuff to save money on overseas letters. Did this stuff even exist anymore?

I open the letter and read.

Paul,
I asked Dad to give you this after I died. I can't believe

I'm dead. I can't believe I just wrote that. I bet you can't believe you just read it. I wish I had something to say to you, Paul, like in the movies. The dead guy always has something to say. But I'm drawing blanks. I'm glad we always got along. We were different, but we were always brothers. I know Dad's an idiot in a brilliant idiot way. He doesn't get it. I know. I've heard you say that a million times. You know what he's said to me a million times? Paul doesn't understand, he's a rock head. Well, you are both fucking rock heads. Do it for Johnny, Paul. You know what I mean. Do it for me. Be Dad's friend for me. I love you, little man.

Bye,
Will

p.s. Got you last.

Bang, bang. My heart races.

"Are you decent?"

I tuck the letter in and close the book and place it back exactly as I found it. I lay my head down, as if his knocking and voice woke me.

"Yes, sorry. Enter."

Paul pushes the door in and then pushes it shut, stepping gently beside my head.

"Sleep is good, but we only have the light for so long. Let's go."

"Where?"

"Up the mountain to the plateau—where we can be seen. It isn't snowing anymore—the weather broke. It's our best chance."

"No. I can't."

I probably can't climb up a mountain, but what's really soul-crushing at the moment is I can't just *do* things without a plan. One day we were making a nest and now he wants to climb a mountain. I feel that old sense of paralysis that's plagued me for years seep into my heart. *Just don't move, Jane. If you don't move, nothing will happen, and that's better than something unexpected happening.*

"You can. You will, unless you want to die alone in a bathroom."

He shuts the door and the tiny echo reverberates a kind of loneliness that's just as terrifying as climbing a mountain.

The ungrateful hardass has returned.

"Wait!" I shout. "Give me a minute and I'll be outside."

I get myself together, glancing briefly at the mirror. It ain't pretty, but hey, there isn't much competition up here.

Paul stands with rope and climbing stuff around his

shoulders. With his sunglasses and gear, he looks a little like a warrior set for battle.

"Let's talk about this for a second," I suggest.

"I'm not wasting time talking about this. Let's go. We'll die down here if we don't. They won't find us until the spring."

"I thought you said two or three weeks?"

"Look." He points up. "The plane landed on a ledge deep in a steep valley in a thick forest of trees. They'll never spot us down here, and if they can't spot us, they won't send a climber blindly into a vast, roadless tundra. We have to be seen."

"But now?"

"Good weather up this high is the anomaly, Jane. This might be our only chance for a week or more."

"Are there no other choices?"

He shakes his head and turns toward a slope that rises a couple hundred yards behind the plane. It doesn't look quite as steep as the rest of the valley for about one hundred feet or so, but then it gets really steep near the top and inverts for about ten feet. It's those last ten feet that make my stomach twist into knots.

"I can't climb that," I say.

"Stop it. You will," he says bluntly.

"I'm not you."

"No, but you'll die here if you don't climb."

"That's nice." I snort.

"It's a fact."

"There are no facts," I shout. I feel trapped and unsure. "You don't know any more than I do. We could be saved in an hour or end up dying on that cliff because of your stupid facts."

Paul's eyes heat up. And then they cool.

"Die, then. It's of no consequence to me. I'm not going to sit here and wait to die; it's not my style."

My heart dries and crumbles in my chest and the tears start to well up. A big, sad lump sags inside my throat. Coldhearted bastard. I hate him. I hate him more than any being I've ever met in my life, including my father, who I've hated since the day he abandoned me. I point to the top of the cliff.

"Don't leave me, Paul," I sob. And then fall to the snow on my knees. He stands over me for a minute as I cry.

"You want me to take you back to the cabin?" he asks.

I nod yes.

"I'm not doing that. That's what the fucking shrinks do, isn't it? Enable you? That's what you call it, right? Well, that's fine in a hospital, where they feed you and take care of you. But not here. Stasis is death."

I hear Old Doctor's voice echoing in Paul's. I stop crying and look up at him and then back at the mountain.

"That invert, I can't do that."

"You're only afraid of what you've never done. You'll do it."

"I'm not afraid; I just can't imagine it's possible."

Paul looks up to the point in the wall where it pops out. "That thing? Oh, that's easier than walking. You can walk, right?"

Sarcasm. That's the answer—a stupid joke. How is it that a boy can go from amazing to jerkhead in a single second?

"I'm going first, so if I fall and die, you can feast on me until help arrives."

He says this with a smile.

"I don't like jerky." So lame, but I had to say something.

"Insulting me won't change anything."

I stand there defiantly. He doesn't say anything and then he looks up to the mountain, like he's thinking about the climb. But just when I'm thinking I took him down a notch or two, he fires back.

"Don't think I don't know your little secret too, Solis. You'd rather give up and be a victim than fight and lose. Easier to cry on daddy's shoulder, isn't it?"

"Screw you," I shout. "My father's dead. And he was a piece of shit, like you."

I push past him. I can't look at his face. I stare up at

the inverted top, trying to will my courage up. I feel like I'm marching right toward the end of my life. How will I ever make it to the top of the mountain?

Why try, I think. Old Doctor's voice echoes in my head: "Because that's what we do. We impose meaning on life."

Inside, something else is bothering me. That word, *victim*. Like a little dagger, Paul stuck me with it. I hate it, but I feel some truth in it. *Fuck him—what does he know about it!*

"Let's go," I say as I brush by him and walk toward the slope.

Chapter 21

We don't speak as we stand at the base of the climb. The weather is just above zero but overcast and the cloud line hovers just above the valley. I feel the sun bearing down from behind the clouds; it casts a slightly ominous light over the valley. The wind pushes us a bit, but there's no snow, except what's kicked up. We couldn't ask for more pleasant conditions, at least by mountain standards.

At the base of the wall, I look up to the top and realize that even the distance we crossed to get here hasn't diminished the steepness and length of the climb. I want to look over at Paul and cry or beg him to turn around, but I push down the impulse. No more crying in front of the Bastard, which is how I will think of him from now on, I decide. I can't give him that satisfaction.

"Listen," he finally blurts out after playing with the ropes for what seems an eternity. "I'm going to lead us up. This is your rope. Run it through your belt loop."

I grab it and pull the rope through my back loop and tie a knot.

"If you fall, that won't hold you," he says.

I look at him with a *so-tell-me-what-to-do-dipshit* stare.

"Pull it through the front and loop the rope around all the loops, like a belt. Then re-loop the last one and tie off a couple of knots. That stitching will hold you. You're like a feather anyway; it won't take much."

Well, at least he noticed! I loop, tie, then nod.

"Let's do it," he says, putting up a fist bump.

"A fist bump," I say. "I'm going to die and you want me to fist bump."

He looks sheepish for a second and then says, "Sorry. Just trying to inspire you. Remember yesterday. You were amazing. Be amazing today."

I look up the mountain one more time to assess my situation. Because the wall in this section is steep, there's less accumulation of snow. That could change in a couple of months, but I'm starting to see the wisdom of Paul's choice. After about one hundred feet of steep hiking, there's a fifteen-to-twenty-foot climb to a small ledge.

Once we make the ledge—and that is if I can make the hundred-foot hike up the icy side of the mountain, followed by the short wall climb—I can see there's an inversion of maybe ten feet that juts out as if Nature herself put it there to prevent all those who have entered this valley from ever leaving. Once over that, we will be off the valley ledge and on the mountain again. From there, maybe—*maybe*—it will be easier for someone to find us.

Paul hands me two one-foot-long sticks, maybe an inch thick, that have been whittled to a sharp point on one end and left untouched at the other.

"For climbing this first bit. Watch me."

He jams the right-hand stick into the snow, which is thick and icy but not impenetrable. His boots are better suited for climbing in snow with their sharp steel toes, and he kicks them into the mountain as well and then jams his left-hand stick a foot or two higher. He starts moving up the mountain, one limb at a time, with slow but remarkable precision.

He turns back and looks at me.

"Come on. Use my toe holes, but make your own stick holes. You'll be fine."

Simple. Just replicate a trained soldier up a mountain. I start to question the validity of this decision. I start to question this whole euphoric feeling I've had since crashing, the adrenaline rush that has picked me up and carried me several times over the last forty-eight hours.

"Come on, Jane. I can't go any higher without you moving behind me."

As a kid—before my father died—I was invited to birthday parties at indoor climbing walls, and I was always drawn to the heights. I was a natural climber and was exhilarated by what I considered the most death-defying climbs. All that went away after he died. I take a breath and try a technique I learned at another hospital from a woman named Dr. Morris, who liked to say, "Visualize who you want to be." I amend her words and try to visualize my younger, more daring self. I watch my younger self dance up the wall like a spider, light and sticky.

I poke my left toe into Paul's first toe hole, leaning my weight against the mountain, simultaneously slamming my right-hand stick into the snow above me. The slope is gradual and supports my body, and the sticks Paul made add balance and grip. I pull up my right boot and find his toe hole again. Holy Jesus, I'm climbing. *Don't look down,* I tell myself. *Don't look down.*

He moves quickly and with purpose up the first fifty feet. Halfway up, he stops and looks down and gives me a thumbs-up. I nod in the most imperceptible way, instinctively, because any energy not going into this climb is wasteful.

Turning back to the mountain, he moves five to seven feet to the right, hand over hand, foot to foot, sideways instead of straight up. When I reach the spot, I see a large splotch of rock-hard ice. It is frozen runoff water from the overhang above it. I shiver for a second, wondering just how far back that ice goes and fearing that the overhang itself could be completely covered.

His sideways steps are long, and it is difficult for me to stretch my legs out wide enough to re-create his steps. I can feel my heart pounding underneath my jacket. My ears ring as my blood surges, and I feel aware of my heart pumping it all through my veins. There's something about moving sideways that makes me look down, and when I do, I feel a rush of dizziness, and the earth below me becomes weirdly elongated. I turn my head back to the mountain, but it's too late. I gag, and bile comes up into my mouth. I spit into the ice in front of me.

"I'm stuck," I shout.

"No you're not."

My body is giving out. I can't move. I can't think. Except I know I've never wanted to slug another human being the way I want to slug Paul Hart right now.

"Because you're me, is that it? You know exactly how it is for me right now." I'm already rattled by the climb, but my anger toward Paul makes me shake even more.

"No, because I know you'll make it," he shouts. I feel a sincere and positive tone in his voice; he's trying to inspire me.

"I can't. I really can't," I shout back. I don't want to be a victim, but I'm stuck and scared. I look down again. We must be sixty or seventy feet off the ground. The slope is so steep, I wonder how we've gotten this far already.

"I'm going to tighten the rope between us and give you a little lift. On the count of three, stretch across."

"I can't," I shout.

"One—"

"No."

"Two—"

"I can't!" I scream, feeling my face burn red as I strain my vocal cords.

"Three."

The rope between us is suddenly taut and I feel my weight lift, and I reach out my right foot and find a new hole and then again with my left. I stop thinking altogether and, foot by foot, I slide across the mountain slope until I reach Paul's new path.

I look up at Paul, who watches me from behind his chrome, mirrored sunglasses, giving me zero to hold onto emotionally.

"What was that?" he hollers down.

"What?"

"I can or I can't?" He laughs.

Bastard. Cambridge-Boston butthead. I focus on the mountain and don't respond. My legs burn, like acid is pumping through my thighs. My arms feel wobbly, like they are made of Play-Doh. I feel doubt blooming in my brain, so I take a few deep breaths and refocus. *Crush the doubts, Jane. They offer nothing and take everything.*

We make our way up, and as Paul hits the first ledge below the wall climb, he pulls me up on the rope as I climb, making my own climb much easier. When I reach the first summit, I lie on my back and stare at the sky for a few minutes. My chest is heaving and my heart is racing, mostly from effort but with some pride too.

"Not bad," Paul says. "Not bad at all."

He stares out over the wall we just climbed and then up the next ascent. I sit up and then shimmy to the edge and put my legs over, letting them dangle.

"Wow. Thank you," I say, trying to find a way to bridge the anger between us.

"Thank yourself." He swipes playfully at the top of my hat and then turns to the wall. He looks up and I follow his gaze. There's nowhere else to go but straight up.

Chapter 22

If it were a sheer wall that required a climbing hammer and those big nails they use, we'd be stuck on this ledge forever. But as I really study it, I can see that the slab of wall isn't smooth but full of cracks, wrinkles, and stubble, like an old man's face.

Paul puts his gloves on the rock and massages the stone. He looks up and to the left, then the right, trying to anticipate the climb, the consequences of choosing each possible path in the stone. For the first time in a while, I look to the sky and see that the dull glow of the sun behind the clouds has moved directly over us. The rock overhang, which I cannot bear to think of, is now directly over us and will be for the rest of the day. If a storm were to come through now, there'd be no way down and no way up. We would surely die up here.

Paul toes his right boot into a crack and then reaches up with his left hand. In a cat-like move, he springs and lifts, and boom, boom, boom, he creeps up the face. In what feels like seconds, he's moved up half the face. He looks down at me and holds up one hand and tells me to stay put.

I watch him with awe. He's studying the rock like a map. There's maybe eight more feet to the next ledge, but it might as well be a mile. He digs into a crack with his right boot and then gracefully reaches up and grabs a knob in the stone with his left hand. He carefully places his left boot against a divot and lifts and then pushes the sole of his right boot against the flat of stone wall, the force holding him there momentarily. And then, with the agility of a monkey, he bounces up and grabs the ledge. He quickly swings his other right hand up, and he's hanging by both arms off the ledge.

For a moment, the air in my lungs rushes out. He dangles a hundred or more feet above the ground, above certain death, if he falls.

If he falls, I selfishly think, *I am dead up here.* I realize, maybe for the first time in my life, that my survival is intimately tied to the survival of another human being. Without him, I will die. With him, there is hope. I can't imagine he feels the same way about me, but then again, without me he'd be frozen in a chair on the side of a cliff.

He pulls himself up, grunting—then shouting—with the effort. He rolls over the ledge and disappears from sight. A few moments later, his buggy mirror sunglasses peep down and he calls, "All right. Don't think about it. It's all instinct."

"I'm not good at instinct. I'm a big over-planner and a great second-guesser," I shout. A little joke, in a difficult moment, isn't so bad, I guess.

He holds up his thumb and grins. "Look who's full of jokes in the panicky moments now."

Then he shouts, "I'm gonna pull you up. Just keep climbing even if you slip."

It's a lot easier to go on instinct when you know whatever you screw up shouldn't matter. *Just keep climbing, Jane. That's the key.*

I address the wall and push the toe of my boot into the crack of the wall, just where he had. I look up one more time for reassurance. Paul isn't where I can see him, but I know he is there, somewhere, lodged against a rock for leverage. I feel a burst of joy inside. Paul is lodged behind a rock; he will not let go; he will pull me up if I fall; no matter what I do, we will find a way. We will get out of here.

I spring up and slot my fingers into the rock with my left hand. I see his path clearly now, and my right hand follows quickly to a knob. My legs feel powerful, springing from one crack to the next, and my hands feel like iron, holding the rock with a grip I did not know I possessed.

I reach the midpoint, where Paul had stopped, and halt my climb. I feel the rope tug on me and I use my left hand to tug back. It goes slack. I stand still and catch my breath, careful not to look down.

"You're amazing, Jane!"

I look up and those bug eyes are watching me.

I look up at the wall. The path that Paul took across the eight remaining feet isn't one I can replicate. His arms are long, and his ability to leap and his upper-body strength far surpass mine. I see a crack in the wall that extends from where I am, zigzagging like a lightning bolt all the way to the top. The problem is that it is another good eight feet to my right.

"If I can get to there"—I shout and point—"can you hold me?"

"Yes. Wait until I give the rope three tugs. That means I'm ready."

I hold up my thumb and wait.

Everything is silent, except for the wind. It sings, a little deathly hollow sound that bounces from rock to rock. It is so lonely, roaming through this valley. I know why that lonely song found its way into my heart before, why the very beauty of loneliness itself could become a friend. It is seductive and sweet, maybe sweeter than anything two people can share. I can still hear the call of it, but it has no pull on me now. I'm just looking at the task in front of me, which is moving eight feet to the left without killing myself.

One, two, three. Paul pulls the rope. I feel it tighten against my waist, and I push off the wall and for a second fly through the air, off the earth and away from its gravity. Then my body comes back against a wall with a smack. I scratch and claw to gain a foothold on the cliff. My pants cinch up tight and stress the loop holes around my rope. I hear one of them tear and suddenly I realize that no matter how strong Paul is, no matter how defined his leverage, if the loops go or the rope goes, I am in big trouble.

My left hand finds grounding first. A little nub my fingers latch onto becomes my lifeline. I pull myself firmly to the wall with all my concentration focused on my index, middle, and ring fingers. My eyes dart up the crack, which is two to three feet to my right now and slightly above my shoulder. I grasp with my right hand and cup the crack where it zigzags back across the face of the mountain. I push to check the firmness of my grip and quickly pull myself up. My feet are still scraping against the rock, but with Paul's pull, they can wait. I reach with my left hand and start hauling myself up the crack.

Suddenly, my right foot finds footing inside the crack and off I go. In a matter of seconds I'm ascending, with Paul's help, up the side and toward the ledge. There's a little abutment of rock sticking out and I can't hoist myself over it. Paul pulls hard, but his force is only pinning me against the rock.

"Stop! Stop pulling!" I can barely call up loud enough for him to hear me.

The rope remains firm but the pulling stops.

"I'm stuck," I call, "beneath a rock."

I can hear Paul make his way slowly toward the edge, probably terrified of being pulled over and having both of us tumble to our doom.

"Jane?"

He's not far from me, but I can't see him because of the rock.

"Yeah?"

"Your rope is jammed in the rock. That's why you can't get onto the ledge." His voice is calm. "We need to cut it."

Cut the rope. The words might as well be *Jane, we need to cut your heart out of your body.* I panic.

"I'll fall!"

"No you won't. Tighten your grip and let me know when the rope isn't supporting you."

I grasp as tightly as I can until I know in my heart that

it is me who is holding my body on this mountain. Not Paul. Not God. Not a rope. Just Jane.

"That's as firm as I can get," I finally call. My voice is cracked. "I'm scared, Paul!"

"I'm gonna cut. You need to hold tight for less than a minute. You can do that. In about thirty seconds, my hand will come down to your left. Reach out and grab it, and I'll pull you up. Trust me. I won't let you go."

"Okay." I say it so softly I'm sure he can't hear.

"Less than a minute," he promises.

I grip with all the force in my being. I think of my angels again, like I'm taking off on a plane. *Hold me here*, I ask. *Hold me on this earth*. I think of my grandfather and my father and my cousin. I imagine their hands on my back, pressing me into the mountainside. Suddenly, I feel light.

"Jane, you're going to have to cut the rope. I can't get the right angle from here."

His hand comes down holding the knife out for me and I reach out and grab it with my right hand.

"You can do this," he says. I can't even spare the energy to answer him.

The line is taut and firm. I push my toes into their hold and jam my left hand as firmly into its hold as I can. I grip the knife and lay the serrated edge against the rope and begin to saw. I am literally pressing my head into the side of the mountain as I saw, trying to keep the rest of my body as still as possible. The blade is sharp, and even though the rope is made to resist fraying, the knife makes its way through. As I near the final threads, I regrip just before snapping the line completely.

It snaps and my weight shifts more than I expect it to. For a second, I wobble. The wind hits me at the same moment and my left foot shifts a millimeter. Reflexively, I thrash out with my right hand and drop the knife. I pull with both hands and cat scratch with my feet, trying to find grounding. I look down and see my boots, the wall, and then one hundred feet of void.

"Grab my hand! Grab my hand!"

I hear Paul shouting. I look to my right and there it is, maybe a foot away. My left hand starts to slip and I flail with my right, over to Paul's, and we grasp just as my left slips free. I'm dangling by one arm over the cliff. Paul's massive hand grips me, but we are suspended in mid-air. All his strength holds me but can't seem to move me up and over.

"Your feet, Jane, get a foothold!"

But my feet are a foot from the wall, swinging wildly in the air. My left hand reaches up and finds a tiny landing on the top of the ledge. I pull as hard as I can, and suddenly, together, Paul and I begin to win the battle. I feel my body moving inch by inch. Paul is screaming like a wild beast, giving everything he has. And then my chest hits the edge and I throw my right leg up and over, landing and rolling onto the ledge.

I let out a scream and pound the ground. I feel like my heart might explode out of my chest, it's throbbing so hard. Paul moves over and rolls me over and wraps his arm around me as tightly as he can. When my ears stop ringing, I realize he is whispering to me.

"It's okay, it's okay, it's okay."

I sob, thinking how close I came to dying, and to pulling Paul over that cliff with me. We lie there for a few moments, just holding each other and catching our breath.

"I dropped the knife," I finally say.

"I know. You couldn't have done anything else."

He looks at the overhang above us and he smiles. "That's okay. We finally caught a break."

Chapter 23

Standing on this tiny ledge, staring up at the inverted overhang that I can't imagine a champion climber ascending, never mind the physically challenged like myself, I am flooded with joy. It comes as I discover for myself that the inverted overhang is split into two distinct pieces of rock.

"You're thinking we can climb through the crack rather than around and over."

"You'll stand on my shoulders and then I'll push your feet up until you can find a grip and pull yourself up," Paul instructs as he scans the crevice. His attention snaps back at me when I don't respond. "Okay?" I nod.

"What happens after?" I ask.

"You'll pull me up or something," he says. "We'll figure it out."

"'Or something' sounds like a great plan," I say.

"It's worked so far."

I don't know how he lives like this. Planless. Instinctive. It drives me nuts, but I bite my tongue.

Paul kneels and I step on his shoulders and hold his hands. He stands up and holds my ankles firmly. I reach up, and my hands feel the bottom of the crack until I'm able to slide my left hand into a hold. I pull, but don't have the strength to lift myself through to a foothold in the crack.

"It's too high," I say.

"Hold on," Paul grunts, and his hands come under my boots and he pushes up with all his might. I reach and stretch until my left hand lands on the floor of the cliff and my right boot finds a foothold. I push hard and Paul gives me one last shove. I hoist my body over the top and land, hard, on the floor, scurrying to pull my legs over.

"I'm over, I'm over," I holler.

"Stay there."

In a matter of minutes, Paul climbs the wall and then shimmies across the crack like he's climbing hand over hand on a pull bar. When he reaches the wide part of the crack, he pulls himself up and over the top.

He stands and looks out over the valley. He has a big smile on his face.

"Not bad, Solis."

He sits down next to me. He puts his hand around my shoulders and pulls me in. My head falls onto his shoulder.

"Yeah, not bad, Hart."

He looks around and then behind us.

"Not exactly what I'd hoped for."

I look around again. My heart sinks. I'm not sure this is the right term for what I'm seeing, but I'm calling it a false top.

We are surrounded by mountain peaks far higher than the one we are standing on. Unless the sky was to turn crystal blue, it's unlikely that a search plane could find us here.

"We can't be found here, can we?" I ask.

"Do you mean alive?"

"Of course."

"Unlikely."

He lies on his back and looks up.

"We have to find shelter, before the sun falls."

I look around and then up toward the sun, or where it should be. I can't believe that we've gone through all of this and haven't changed our situation at all. Except, of course, that we no longer have the bathroom shelter. A cold wind hits my face and I turn into Paul's chest to protect myself.

"Don't freak out on me now," Paul whispers in my ear.

"I'm not." I sit back up. "It's the wind; it surprised me."

He sits up and puts both arms around me, pulls me in tight, and kisses the top of my head.

"The worst is below us now," he says. "Look."

I don't look, because I know looking back is a haunting feeling all its own.

I made it up the cliff and I feel good about that, but I'm still terrified of what's to come. If I add obsessing about my near-death climb into the mix, I'll end up a morass of nerves.

"I'm scared," I say with honesty.

"I nearly shit my pants back there. It's okay to be scared."

"That's what they tell me."

"Who's they?" Paul asks.

"People."

"Doctors, you mean?"

"Yes, doctors, parents, friends, and now strange boys I meet on mountaintops. But everyone tells me to walk around like there's nothing to be afraid of. Then they drop dead or something."

"I'm sorry about that quip, about daddy's girl."

"You didn't know."

"It's funny how people just drop dead one day. My mom died when I was ten. I remember the scent of her hair. Strawberries. That's what I remember most about her."

"My dad shot himself in the head. I just think about blood when I think about him. He used Old Spice. Blood and Old Spice. That's what I remember."

We just stand there for a few moments taking in each other's histories. We are so different and yet so alike, I think. We both lost a parent.

"Do you suppose they think we're dead?" He breaks the silence.

"I don't know, but I think my mother would be pleased I finally met a guy."

Paul laughs out loud.

"Did you find a guy, Solis? That's nice to know."

Chapter 24

Less than an hour later, in the middle of a crop of slab-like stones, we find a small cave. Inside, the ground is dry and the wind is blocked. It is short and tapered, so we have to have our heads at the entrance.

"As good as it gets," Paul says after inspecting the cave.

I can feel the cold air circulating around the opening of the cave and I fear the exposure could be too much.

"Is it enough?" I ask.

"It has to be. It's all we've got."

We unroll our sleeping bags and lay them side by side. Our shelter is snug and the ceiling at the apex couldn't be more than four feet.

"Take off your boots and socks and gloves," Paul says.

"Socks in your bag, boots underneath. Put on the dry pair; we'll rotate each day if we can."

I nod in agreement.

"We'll get in my bag, then pull this one over our heads. It'll be warmer this way. Unzip the jacket so our bodies will heat each other more efficiently."

My embarrassment hardly registers. I do everything he's asked and slide down into the bag. He's opened his jacket and I can feel the warmth off his chest. He reaches down into the bag behind himself and pulls out the two plastic soda bottles he had underneath his jacket all day.

"Did they melt?"

"Mostly, yes."

I take a long pull from the first bottle. And then a short follow-up. I hand it back, knowing he must be dying of thirst too.

"Sorry. I didn't realize how thirsty I was."

"It's okay, but don't drink too fast—when you're this thirsty, you can heave it back up. That wouldn't be good."

He takes a long pull himself and hands it back to me. "Good system; I'll refill in the morning."

I take a few more swigs, feeling the water flood through my body, and then, reluctantly, I hand it back so he can finish it off. Hunger kicks in as I watch him finish the water.

"We have Raisinets and three energy bars, right?" he asks.

"Yes."

"So let's eat the Raisinets and we split one bar a day."

"But you're so much bigger, it doesn't seem fair," I say.

"Honorable of you, but I'm fine."

He's reaching into his bag, and for a moment, I think he's going to ask me which kind of bar we should choose to eat tonight, but he doesn't. He just rips one open, breaks the bar in two pieces that are roughly the same, and hands one half to me.

"Cheers!"

"Eat slow," I say. "That's what my mom would tell me."

"I miss my mom. I would fight and scream about cleaning up my room. Then she died and I missed how much she took care of everything."

"How did she die?"

"Cancer. Breast cancer. Her dad was a two-pack-a-day man."

"Sorry," I say. "What about your dad?"

"My dad didn't care about anything after my mom died. He threw himself into his books and work and left my brother and me to fend for ourselves. There were weeks at a time when Will, he's my brother—he's dead too—cooked dinner. We only knew how to make two things: grilled cheese and scrambled eggs."

"That sounds horrible. I mean about Will too; I'm so sorry."

"Cancer. I prayed for him every night and day and absolutely nothing happened. He wasted away in less than a year."

I stare at him. It is dark, so I'm not sure he can see me, but I'm sure he senses me.

"It wasn't so bad before he got sick. My dad and Will, they got along. Will loved to read what dad was reading. I hated reading. I'm dyslexic or I was, and was probably ADD, too."

I touch his back and tell him I'm sorry.

"We haven't spoken in two years. My dad and I. I was flying home to see him."

"Why?"

"Was I flying home?"

"No, why haven't you spoken to him?"

"Will died," he said, and there was a pause and what I thought was a little sniffle, but maybe not. "And I didn't want to go to college. My dad said I couldn't stay home and live with him. If I wasn't going to school and seeing a shrink with him, I'd have to make it on my own. So

I went to the shrink with him for a year or so and the doctor sided with my father on everything. I mean he didn't say it directly like that, but everything always got twisted up and about me. And just before I left for good, we had a session where Dr. Klein, that was his name, kept hounding me about doing homework and chores and whatever my dad wanted me to do and I exploded. I jumped at him, but my dad held me back. After that I just left."

Paul shifts his arm and reaches out and touches my face, then my hair.

"Sorry," he says, "I need to know where your face is; I was disoriented."

"It's okay. It felt nice," I say.

He strokes my face and hair again.

"I flew out west with the money I had. I work as a ski instructor in the winter. In summer I surf in Cali. That was almost two years ago."

"And you've never spoken?"

"Nope."

"Nothing—not a text?"

"An email once every six months or so. We're like that; the Harts are sort of brutal. My grandfather once made my father spend an entire summer pulling rocks out of the yard because he got a C on his report card. Each day, as the story goes, my dad squared off six by six feet of yard and on his hands and knees picked out every stone and rock under the turf. It took him sixty-six days to finish it off. When he was done, he brought my grandfather the bucket of stones and my grandfather tossed them into a river and then said, 'Study harder next time,' and walked away."

"Wow." I think about it. "My mother never punished me, really, for anything."

"I suppose he had it tough," Paul says, placing his whole hand on my cheek. "But he was worse on me. His dad, at least, gave a damn."

We settle in and finish off the Raisinets. My stomach roars with the expectation of more food. Paul's is even louder, and I feel a tinge of guilt over splitting the food evenly.

Total darkness descends quickly and the wind picks up, howling past us, but our cave provides a lot of protection. There's a long stretch of silence, his warm breath on my neck. I'm afraid to speak, to say the wrong thing after his confession. My head throbs and muscles I didn't even know I had are aching. My head feels weirdly off-kilter.

Paul grasps my left hand and for a split second, I know he can feel the scars from where I tried to hit the switch last year.

"I'd never ask," he whispers.

"I know. I know you wouldn't."

"I don't like knowing other people's shit."

"I can tell. You're too mean."

"Am I?"

"I think you threatened to leave me for dead back there."

"I did, didn't I?"

"Yes."

"But I melted water for you and you did end up climbing a really big-ass mountain."

"Yes," I say, squeezing his hand.

He holds my other hand in his and he squeezes back. Not in a stay-warm kind of way, but more in the I-like-you kind of way. Maybe these aren't the best conditions to try to discern those types of messages, what with the weather, the medication withdrawal, the hunger, the layers of random outerwear, and the darkness, but I feel a change in the air and something like affection rises in me.

"I was turning fifteen," I say into the darkness. "I had lived in New York City my whole life, but we had just moved to New Jersey. My father had been dead for nearly four years and money was tight, or that's how my mom would describe it. And that didn't matter. None of it did. I'd never had many friends anyway. I'd been a loner since high school started."

I stop talking for a minute. Paul doesn't say anything, but he puts his left hand through my hair and I can hear his heartbeat. I take a deep breath. Then he stops.

"You don't have to talk about it."

"No one's ever touched them before. I mean nobody I didn't pay to touch them."

"You employed some male hookers to touch your scars?"

I laugh. The dumb jokes are starting to grow on me.

"Yeah, I liked to make them dress up like doctors."

He laughs. "You're funny, for a girl."

"Most girls are," I say.

"You're probably right," he whispers. "That's the kind of thing my dad would say. I hate when I sound like him."

I clear my throat and think about the words I want to use. I think about how my first impulse is always to lie or obfuscate the truth, but how with Paul I just want everything to be honest and straightforward.

"Let me start over. My father shot himself on Christmas Eve. He didn't just die—that's how I talk about it, like he died the way people normally die. My great-grandfather hit the switch too, and my grandmother spent the last decade of her life in a house for crazy women in Vermont. My dad never told me this, but my mom let me know after he died that his mother killed herself inside that home—she hung herself. Being crazy is a family hobby." I laugh a little as I say this.

"Well," he says, interlocking our fingers. "I guess we've gotten kicked around by the same shit, in a way."

"Yeah, I guess," I say.

He leans in and kisses my forehead. "I'm sorry. I really am."

"Thanks," I whisper. I feel a flood of emotion come up and settle in my throat and chest.

"It was the beginning of September and I was standing in the kitchen, making lunch. I started slicing some tomatoes. There was something about the way the knife went through the skin of the tomato that caught my eye. Then, in a moment of what felt like crystal clarity, I decided to slice my fingers and then my palm. The first cut felt like euphoria. Then the blood poured out of me, and it felt like liquid relief as every ounce of anxiety burst out of my veins. Blood was everywhere but I didn't care, and then I made the cut you just traced with your fingers. It could have killed me, but my mother came in and stopped me."

"Were you really trying?"

"That's the big question, isn't it?"

"I suppose it is."

"I don't remember."

"Bullshit."

I'm silent for a while.

"How very Hart of you," I say. "That's sort of harsh to say to someone."

"Wouldn't you be happier if you owned up to it and moved on? Whether you were serious or not doesn't matter, really."

I want to be mad and angry, but I can't ignore the blunt truth, that I think he's right.

"The other night on the plane," he said, "were you going to cut yourself too?"

I shake my head. "No. Pills. A concoction of things I researched and put together. They spilled on the floor during the crash before I had taken very many."

I stop talking. I am unable to speak as the enormity of what has happened—what could have happened—hits me.

Then Paul lightly touches my neck with his fingertips and gently pulls me to him. He kisses me. His lips are open and wet. My mouth opens and our lips slide together without hesitation. Then he pulls back for a moment, and we lock eyes. In that instant I know he knows my heart. He kisses me again. I can't speak. I can barely think. My body tingles with hope and lust and love and desire.

We kiss over and over again, and then he gently bites on my ear. I want to explode out of this bag. I turn toward him, ignoring the pain that shoots through my back when I move, and our legs get all tangled up. He kisses my mouth and I hear a rushing sound in my head. My left arm reaches around and underneath his shirt, rubbing his hip bone and belly. He groans softly. And then just as suddenly, the day weighs on me and I curl deeper into his body and hold his hands and arms against my body. He kisses my neck a few more times, and then we fall asleep.

Chapter 25

I dream. I am in the hospital and Old Doctor stares at me, but when he talks, I hear my mother's voice. He asks me the same question over and over, like he doesn't hear me. Finally I scream.

"You don't fool me! You don't fool me!"

Old Doctor stands and walks to the window. He stares out into the courtyard for a moment and then he turns back to me and beckons me to come over. I do and it immediately starts to snow and I smile.

"What are you smiling about, Jane?" he asks.

"The snow—it's beautiful."

He looks outside and then says: "What snow? There's no snow, Jane. You know that, right?"

"You're a liar," I say.

He just smiles, and suddenly my mother is sitting next to him, and my dead father and grandmother are off in the distance, making snow angels.

"Can I play?" I ask.

"No," Old Doctor says, shaking his head, still smiling. My mother cries. And Old Doctor puts his arm around her. He whispers something in her ear and she nods. He kisses her on the cheek, and I want to kill him for my father. She digs in her purse and pulls out my father's watch, hands it to me, and tells me not to lose it again. I get up and walk toward Dad and Grandma, and by the time I reach them, they are gone. The snow angels are there, and their eyes come alive and then they fly away. I look up to watch them, and then my father is standing next to me and I'm opening and closing his watch over and over again. Then Paul walks toward us. But he is dead. I try to reach out and touch him, but there is glass between us. I smash my hands against the glass over and over and scream his name.

His eyes open and he says, "Tell me the truth?"

"About what?"

But his eyes close before I can speak and I know he is dead again.

"Hey, sleepy," Paul says, shaking my shoulder.

"Yeah."

"Are you okay?"

"Why?"

"You're hitting me."

"You're here," I say, half stunned, half asleep.

"Well, yeah." He leans over and kisses me. I remember last night again and then I kiss him back, putting both hands to his face. He breaks it off.

"Stay here," he says, "I'm gonna go scout our next move."

I nod, and almost in an instant, he slips from the bag into the woods. It happens so fast that for a minute I wonder if I'm dreaming, and I scramble out of the bag to go after him.

"Wait," I shout. "Paul! Paul!" But no answer comes. I shout again. Silence. *Trust, Jane. Trust. He would never leave you. But what if it's not up to him?* I shove my feet into my boots and get my gloves and shell and the little second-guesser in my head rises, fresh and alert, like she's just risen from her own nap. He could just keep walking or fall in a lake; what if his foot is stuck in a bear trap or he tumbles off a cliff? *Stop! Quiet the voice, Jane. Focus on what is real. Focus on what you can control.*

I roll up the extra sleeping bag, my hand caressing the warmth that remains where our bodies were. I play back every detail from the night before. The kisses and touches tumble together in my mind and I smile. My dream, my dream, for the life of me it has disappeared in a matter of seconds. I try to catch it, but all I remember is his face in the window, waving goodbye.

My hand finds his little book at the bottom of his sleeping bag, the one his brother gave him. I pick it up and feel the cover. I slide back in the sleeping bag and then open the book and pull out the letter I read once before and snuggle into the bag where I'm hidden in case Paul reappears.

I read it again, with what I now know about Paul and his life after his mother died. What was Will trying to tell him?

I fold the letter up and place it carefully back inside and close the book.

Then guilt grows inside me; perhaps I shouldn't have read his brother's letter. *Hold it! I definitely shouldn't have read his letter!* It is so wrong to be reading Paul's private things. If he found out, would he ever forgive me?

I crawl back out of the bag and switch out what I can for drier things. I pack up. I grab the water bottles and pour the last drop or two onto my tongue. Then I pack them with snow and place one down my jacket and slide it over to the small of my back. Damn, that's cold. I roll our bag up and crawl out into the forest.

He is standing a few feet from the cave, looking at the mountains.

"Do you know where we are?"

"I'm not sure I do. But I think if we can climb up that peak, there's none higher. We'll be able to see the world below, and, hopefully, they will be able to see us."

"Is it possible?"

He shrugs as if to say he doesn't know for sure.

"Anything is possible," he finally says. "You just have to get yourself to believe it first."

Chapter 26

I look out over the range above and before us. I see where we need to go, but I don't see how to get there.

"Look over there." Paul points.

I look. I see a sea of trees and some hills and then a deep gully separating our peak from the higher peaks.

"I don't see what you are looking at," I say.

He comes and holds my arm, pointing it toward a speck on the horizon. "There," he says, guiding my hand with his.

I realize that he is pointing down. Down into the next valley, then up.

"All the way down?" I say.

"No, see there," he says. "There's a natural bridge connecting the two peaks. It could be dangerous, but I feel like it's our best shot."

"How far is that?"

"I don't know. Should take us a day or so to get there."

I have no idea if he's kidding. I'm trying to imagine how we'll ever be found. Maybe twenty years from now, the wreckage will be located and our bodies found frozen under ten feet of snow. Actually, that's unlikely, because the bears will never let us sit that long once they wake up in the spring. We'll be tasty morsels once the snow melts.

"Down and up again," I say.

"Yes," he says. "On the upside, no cliffs to climb."

"And the weather, let's be thankful for that."

"That's the spirit, Solis. Yes, the weather is almost a balmy zero degrees today."

You couldn't really see it from where we stood, but somewhere off in the distance, the sun must be shining brightly behind the mountains. We are still under a canopy of tall trees, but the air is warmer. I do feel hopeful.

"I'm guessing it'll take us the day to get down and another day to get back up. Once there, if the weather holds, we'll try to start a fire."

"What will we eat?" I ask.

He looks at me strangely, and then he says, "I'm more

worried about what we'll talk about. We can go without food for days; plus we've still got some candy. We've got water, too. But after our conversation last night, I fear there's nothing left to confess."

"Really, that's your fear? Running out of confessions?"

"I'm afraid so."

He looks around at our stuff and he starts feeling his jacket and checking his pockets.

"What are you looking for?"

He looks at his bag and my things.

He's starting to panic me, so I ask again. "What's missing?"

"My book," he finally says.

"Your book, it's in there," I say, pointing at the sleeping bag on his back.

There's a long pause between us and he's looking at me, reading my body language. I'm covered head to toe in jackets, sunglasses, gloves, and a hat, so I can't imagine there's much to read.

"Did you read the letter?" he snaps.

"No," I say. It is reflexive, but I immediately regret lying.

"Really?" he says skeptically.

"I started it. I'm sorry."

"Right. You didn't inhale all the way either," he says

with a smirk. "Why do you lie so much? Why would you read something so personal without asking?"

"What? I wasn't thinking. It was before I knew you. I mean, knew you like I know you now."

"Never mind, Solis, let's go."

Chapter 27

The hike down into the valley is difficult. It is also silent. Whatever passed between us the night before has evaporated, and hardass Paul has reappeared again, but this time there's anger in his voice. I read his letter, and now he resents my very presence on this mountain.

"Keep up," he shouts sharply every couple of minutes.

His pace is fast and purposely punishing. Plus, I'm stiff from yesterday. I don't hear any playfulness—even compassion—in his voice. On the cliff yesterday, even when he was brutally tough on me, his voice always had a sense of kindness, or at least I'd thought it did. But now I just feel something different emanating from him: a seething, righteous anger. He hates me. It appears reading his brother's letter was an unforgivable offense. And I agree with him.

There's only one benefit to all of this, which is that my head is so singularly focused on Paul and his mood that I'm actually ignoring the deep hunger in my stomach, the blisters on my feet, and the weakness in my legs.

"Look there," I say.

Paul stops. He turns to me.

"What?"

"There, on the tree? Somebody carved a triangle into the tree with a knife. That's a sign, right?"

He turns quickly and stares for a second at the tree and the triangle. Despite his efforts to hide it, a big grin spreads across his face.

"Holy shit," Paul shouts. "We've got a trail!"

He turns to throw his arms around me, but then he catches himself midway, remembering his anger.

His hands fall to his sides and his smile fades.

"It might mean something. It might not."

I nod. He's right, and anyway, even this great stroke of luck can't turn his heart back toward me. I feel a sob in my throat, but I will not show him how he is hurting me. I just mouth, "Right."

"We'll follow the trail down a bit," he says. "But it's heading in the wrong direction if we want to cross the bridge. It might be easier walking, but it's going to take us to the bottom of the valley. That's a death march. We'd never make it back up."

I regain my composure and take a deep breath as if I'm contemplating the landscape with him, but I'm honestly just checking the emotions roiling through my body. *I am,* I remind myself, *coming off my meds. I might be super-sensitive right now and attributing thoughts and feelings to him that are completely products of my own anxiety.* And then I hear the Old Doctor: *Push the voices aside, Jane; stop the second-guessing. Do what's in front of you and focus on your true voice.*

"I think there's a reason people have set a marker here," I say to him. "I think there's a reason we're seeing this."

"Like God sent it to us." Paul smiles condescendingly. "Lot of good *that* did us on the plane."

"We're still here, aren't we?"

"Thanks to what—random seat placement? I certainly wasn't the one praying or only you'd be here," Paul says. I hate when he's right and logical.

"Nobody knows anything, Paul."

"Here's what I know," Paul says in a low, angry growl, like he's letting out a decade of anger at the world, but at me because I'm the closest one to him. "God isn't here. And he wasn't in that plane. He wasn't there when my mom or Will died or your dad whacked himself. He wasn't there for Margaret or the captain or the others. And let's say he was here, what made us so special? We're a suicidal and an atheist, right? Why save us? Here's the only truth I can be certain of right now: There's a cold, icy world on the top of this mountain. Fall, you die; eat snow, you die; if you're not found, you die. Those are the facts and God isn't going to swoop in and change that. And just because there's a triangle on a tree, carved by who knows who and who knows when, doesn't mean it is going to lead us out of here. In fact, it could lead us down there to our deaths or back around from where we just came. Sometimes signs are just signs; sometimes they lead you in the wrong direction."

There's a long silence between us. I hate him for giving voice to a deep-seated doubt about the world that has lived inside me since the day my father offed himself. Relentless. Cold. Brutal. Doubt has no antidote, except maybe on days when you climb a mountain.

"I get it, Paul. My father's dead and your brother's dead, and nothing is changing that." I stand there, directly in front of him. I don't know where those words came from, but there they are, settling in the space between us, a swirl of words instead of snow. And then I add, "I'm wrong about a lot, and God knows I'm not a poster child for mental health, but I know a few things. Pain isn't good, but it isn't bad either. Hiding it, nurturing it—that's what's bad. That's what I've been doing for years. And it's toxic, rotting me from the inside out. But it's rotting you too. You can't hide from your father and use your brother's and mother's death as an excuse to do it."

Rage fires his eyes for a moment and I fear for myself for just a second. I've gone too far. But the truth in it is pure. I can't deny it.

"Just because you stole and read my brother's letter doesn't mean I fucking want to talk with you about it."

"Have you asked yourself why you kept leaving that 'fucking' book out beside me?"

"Oh, is that the kind of thing you learned from your shrink?" He practically spits.

There's a quiet between us that's deep and still. He turns away and looks at the carved sign again. His body shakes with anger, but he doesn't say anything else. *Don't say anything, Jane.* I put my hand on his shoulder, but he shrugs me off immediately. *Stand down, Jane.*

"We'll stay off trail."

"Okay," I say. "I'm sorry."

"Don't be. Let's go."

An hour later, we near the bridge and we've made good time. The sun is high up in the sky, hidden behind a stampede of rolling white clouds coming down from the north. White and dense, they're not storm clouds, but they keep the sun from warming us. The air temperature hovers around zero.

We push through dense brush, and there are thickets and prickers hiding under the snow that make walking very difficult.

The snow isn't deep here because of a weird combination of the steepness of the mountain and the thick canopy of brush and leaves that cover the ground. But every step brings a new scratch on my legs, neck, or face. I try to bring my scarf up over my face, but it keeps getting caught and tangled. I put my arm across my nose, tucking it into my elbow, and use my other arm to separate and move through the bushes. Paul has been trudging through first, which is helpful, but there's always backlash, and the moment he clears a path, it closes. I can only see two to three feet in front of me, and I realize that I'm essentially on my own. But unlike my initial foray up the cliff yesterday, I don't feel an overriding sense of fear. I've survived worse already, and I can suffer the thorns and branches of this forest.

At one point, I hear a rustling below me, and I see a small rabbit caught under the pressure of a branch that my boot has just landed on. It is enough to pin the white rabbit into the snow, where she must have hidden herself. Her reddish eyes shine at me. I see terror, but I also see food.

I reach into the pocket of my coat and pull out one of the climbing sticks Paul carved for me the day before. I can feel the rabbit squirming even more. *She must sense my thoughts,* I think. *She must know I aim to kill her and eat her.* The thought of it makes my mouth salivate with hunger. I press down as hard as I can with my boot and I hear a little screech.

I raise the stick in the air and I plunge it into the neck of the rabbit and blood spurts out onto the snow. It struggles wildly for a second and then it lies flat. I reach inside my pockets and pull out one of the plastic bags we'd taken to keep stuff dry. I pick up the rabbit and toss it into the bag. I look at the blood on my hands and remember the day when my own blood covered my hands and arms. *I did try to kill myself,* I think. I've known the answer to Old Doctor's question all along: The first time I tried to commit suicide wasn't just a practice run. It was a step on a ladder. Dark seeds had been planted long ago on that Christmas Eve; and with each daydream and thought and, eventually, my practice runs, I climbed closer to killing myself. Had I not dreamed of copying my father or made those small cuts that first day, I could not have gotten on that plane with a handful of pills.

But I guess the opposite is true too: had I not taken

that first step, I would not be who I am now: a fighter. I make a small promise to tell Old Doctor just that if I ever get out of here. "But why? That's the question," he'd say.

My thoughts are interrupted by a bloodcurdling yell, followed by a heavy thud. My adrenaline spikes and I run as fast as I can, crashing through the brush. A thorn rips across my face. I feel blood drip down my face and I lick it instinctively. It is salty and thick with iron.

I'm listening for Paul but hear no further screams or movement as I fight through the thick brush. A pricker bush hidden in the middle of the patch grabs hold of my jacket and yanks me back. The fabric tears, and I stop and slowly disentangle myself. The thorns lie deep in the shell. As I pull them out, feathers and stuffing follow. It takes more than a minute to pull free of everything.

Once free, I step backward out of the bush and move around it slowly, careful not to snag my jacket again. I push through a small clump of baby spruces, and that's when I see what Paul did not: a hidden drop of about twenty or thirty feet. The jagged edges of the snow cover below betray what must be a bed of stones at its base. My knees buckle, and I have to reach out and grab a tree to keep myself from falling.

Paul lies on the ground below, his body twisted in an unnatural way. He must have come through the bushes too quickly and missed the drop they concealed. The snow can play tricks on your eyes that way, leveling out the dips and drops. White on top of white becomes a constant. And eventually, if you're tired or distracted or both, the ground blends into a smooth, flat landscape.

"Paul!" I scream. My voice echoes through the valley. He lies like a dead deer next to a pile of stones. Blood is splashed brightly against the snow. I look down at his lips and hands and boots, but there's no movement at all.

"Paul!" I shout again. The silent, lonely echo reverberates around the valley bottom and back again.

I look left, then right, and find, not more than seven feet to my right, a steep but manageable path down to where Paul lies. The randomness of it all, our crash, our survival, the near misses climbing the cliff the day before, and now the single misstep that caused Paul to fall fifteen feet into a bed of rocks, defies logic. There's no rhyme or reason to life, despite my deepest hopes that I'll find one. Why wasn't his jacket caught in the prickers like mine? Was he careful to avoid them and now lies dead because of it? Why didn't I die?

I scurry down as fast as I can, reaching Paul in a matter of minutes.

I pull off my gloves and touch his face with my hands. Warm. I feel his neck for a pulse and then place my index finger beneath his nose. Warm breath flows onto my fingers. I lean down and kiss his head.

"Paul," I say, gently slapping his cheek.

He stirs but looks glassy-eyed and dull, like a baby who has eaten too much sugar.

"Paul!" I shout at him. "Can you hear me?"

His eyes focus a little and I stroke his hair.

"What happened?" His question is more a croak.

"You fell."

I sit back on my knees and look down at his body. His right arm is bent backward. My stomach twists at the sight of the unnatural line of the bone. I have to put my hand up to cover my mouth. There's nothing there, but my muscles strain to release drips of bile.

"Fix me?" he says calmly. "You can do it; I'll show you."

I'm not sure what to do, but I nod assuredly. "Of course."

"Find two straight branches, very straight. No, make it four. And give me all your sleeping pills or whatever you were taking. The ones you were going to kill yourself with."

I hesitate for a moment and then reach into my pockets and pull out whatever is left. It is a good pile: enough to knock somebody out for a long while. Not enough to off him, but probably enough to get through whatever we have to get through.

I hand them to him and I remove a bottle with melting snow from underneath my jacket. He opens his mouth and I pour a bunch of pills onto his tongue and then help him as best I can with the water. A lot of it spills, which pains me, but I ignore it and slowly he swallows the pills. He falls back and groans from the pain, and I realize that's my signal to find the branches.

I look around and realize Paul's fall has brought us to the base of the bridge that connects the two valleys. If Paul can survive this, we are close to making our way home. *We have to survive,* I tell myself.

The woods are thick, but not impenetrable. Breaking off the branches from a live tree proves to be difficult for me. Some of the branches are too thick and provide too much resistance and the very breakable ones are simply too thin to serve as splints.

I walk into the woods, looking for fallen trees or branches. Fifty feet in, I look back and realize I am farther away from Paul than I've been since the ascent. My boot prints disappear under the shrubbery. I think of shouting to him, but I realize I'm on my own at this point. It's up to me. He will need me now to leave this valley.

I stop for a moment and take stock of everything. I close my eyes and try to imagine the trail back to Paul. *I know where I am,* I think. I open my eyes and kneel in the snow, looking at the trail of steps I have just taken, and I visualize myself walking back to Paul.

I keep moving forward until I find a clearing with a fallen pine. It looks like it has been lying here for a while. I walk to the top end, where the branches are younger and thinner. I break off four sturdy branches and head back to Paul, following my prints, still fresh in the snow.

I think about one therapy session with Old Doctor when the trees were just beginning to bud, so it must have been early spring.

"You like to read, Jane?" Old Doctor asked.

"Yes, but not if you tell me what you want me to read."

"I see. I'm the same way."

"Good."

"But," he mumbles.

I couldn't take it. "Always a 'but' with you people. I wish you would just say what you want to say. Always a bait and switch. I'm just like you, BUT. I like movies myself too, BUT . . ." (Of course, this was early on, before I got the hang of what was needed to manage Old Doctor.)

"You're right, Jane."

"But? Come on, what's the BUT?"

"No, no. You're right."

We sat there staring at each other for about a minute, maybe two, and I waited for his qualification. I thought if

I spoke, he might be able to dodge it and make his point with some other turn of phrase. If I waited, I knew, he would undoubtedly provide it.

"Emerson believed that all the human world could be explained, in Nature, if one sat long enough, patiently enough, with enough focus and insight to pull the lessons from beneath the hard bark of an old tree."

"What the hell is that supposed to mean?"

"I like the sound of it."

"You want me to read him? Emerson?"

"Not really, not unless you're interested."

We sat again in silence. His watery-blue eyes had no emotion on the surface, but in that moment I thought about all the tears, shame, anger, and misery they had probably witnessed. I wondered if he absorbed all the pain he listened to. Then I snapped out of it.

"Double reversing now. I am not falling for it," I finally said with a smirk and a great deal of satisfaction.

"I am not your enemy, Jane."

"Are you in charge of when I can get out of this place?" I asked. "Because, actually, I think you might be."

He smiled.

"You are the most important person in this process." He said this calmly. It bugged me that he wasn't getting really angry.

"So I could be at home studying a tree in my own back-yard." I snorted. "Is that what you have my mother paying you the big bucks for? So you can tell all of us trapped people to go out and contemplate trees?"

"I was offering up something for your further thought or meditation, in response to your suspicion about our conversation."

"Bullshit," I said, looking right at him. I knew he was being honest, but backing down would be too embarrass-ing.

"Our time is up for today."

"You always have that trick."

"I suppose we both do."

Chapter 28

I follow my path in the snow back to Paul quite easily and find him sleeping. I lay the branches down on the ground and shake him gently. He comes to fairly quickly.

"You can't sleep now," I tell him.

He looks at me dully, the information not processing through his brain as quickly as normal.

"Right," he says, "should stay awake after a head injury."

He looks at the pile of branches.

"You've taken a lot of pills, Paul. I'm going to have to wake you every hour or so, just to be safe."

"Take off the branches and find the straightest one," he whispers.

I pick out two short, thick pieces and pull off the small branches.

"Okay," Paul says. "Make my arm straight like yours and then lay it between these branches. Then wrap one of the extra shirts around it as firmly as you can and tie it off."

"I can't straighten your arm."

He ignores me. I take a sideways look at Paul's arm. It looks fine through to the elbow, but then a little more than halfway down the forearm, it breaks the wrong way. Even underneath his jacket, the angle is profoundly distorted.

"Put your hands on my arm, as gently as you can."

I place my hand on the top part of his arm.

"Undo the snap by my wrist, gently, please." I can't believe I am going to do this, but I know that I need to save him and I think that—to save myself—I need him.

I pull his jacket sleeve open, and Paul winces with pain but nods at me to keep going. I can see the sweat building up on his forehead.

"Pull back the jacket sleeve, and the sweater and the turtleneck." He shuts his eyes as I begin and adds, "As carefully as you can, please."

As I pull back his jacket sleeve, the bulge from the broken bone protrudes more clearly, the thin underlayers holding the form of it. Paul muffles deep, painful groans by biting on the outside of his left jacket sleeve. But he can't suppress a yelp of pain when I begin to pull back the tight-fitting turtleneck sleeve. There's blood staining the sleeve, and I realize part of the way down that a little piece of the bone is sticking into the fabric, holding the sleeve to his forearm.

"I'm so sorry!"

"Aahhhh!" he screams. He pounds his good fist against the snow two or three times, screaming, "Fuck!" I stop pulling and watch his sleeve for a bit as a little more blood pools into the cloth.

"Leave it on. Leave it on." He pounds his fist twice more and then looks at me with wild and alert eyes.

"Do it, Jane . . . set it now!" he commands.

"I can't hurt you!" I shout.

"Just push the bones together and get them as straight as you can. Put them between the sticks and wrap it up as tightly as you can. Please, Jane!"

In a swift motion, I grab his arm and push the bone back down into what I hope is its proper place. Paul screams like a wild animal caught in a trap and then goes silent, slumping to the ground. His shrieking rings in my ears.

I say his name, but he doesn't respond. Pain, of the severe and unrelenting variety, can cause people to pass out or numb up. Or it could just be the full load of pills kicking into his system. I look at his arm again, and it is straight now, but still twisted so the hand doesn't face the right direction. I hold the forearm steady in my left hand and turn the wrist and the hand into place. The sound of bones crunching is stomach-turning.

I slide the flattest branch under the arm and then I place two skinny straight ones on either side. I take one sweater sleeve and put it under the forearm right at the elbow and slowly wrap it around and around, as tightly as I can manage, until it reaches his wrist. I grab the fourth stick and slide it in between his arm and the flattest piece of wood, creating a splint to keep the hand from dangling.

I look at Paul and he's still out cold from the pain and probably the pills. I look up and see that the day is almost over. I look around and try to imagine what he would decide to do. First shelter, that's number one. Then water. I pull out the bottle of melting snow from between my back and jacket. Then I feel for his, lifting up his jacket to pull out the pouch of water.

When I push my hand up under his jacket, I feel a swollen lump on his ribs right beside the bottle. I touch his ribs gently, following the laceration and the bump, from the left side of his rib cage all the way to the front near his heart. I wonder if his ribs are broken too.

What if he dies? Please don't die.

"Don't second-guess, Jane," I could hear the Old Doctor

speaking. "It's neither helpful nor worthy of your time." *Focus, Jane.* I look around again and quickly head back toward the dense forest with the fallen tree. I find the tree and gather as many dried-out branches as I can break and carry.

It takes five trips, but eventually I carry enough to where Paul is lying and make a pile. I open both sleeping bags and cover Paul up while he sleeps. I look up to the sky—for help, I guess. Maybe just pity. Maybe just for an acknowledgment that I'm not alone. But no magical voice shouts down with wisdom from the heavens. It might as well be dead up there. All the living is being done down here.

I look at Paul sleeping and realize how little use he will be going forward. A broken arm, a head wound, and, possibly, crushed ribs: there is no way he's going to be able to climb out of here.

I gather stones from the pile Paul landed on to make a bed for a fire. Then I make a little grid of the thinnest and driest branches. I go into Paul's knapsack and pull out his dry matches and his brother's diary. I open it and pick up the letter and reread it.

Tears come to my eyes and I choke up. I think of what Paul and his father are tossing away, but I know it is no worse than what my father stole from me and his mother stole from him. I stuff the letter in my pocket for safety and wipe away my tears on my sleeve. I promise myself I won't knowingly hurt another soul if I can get this fire started.

Then I go to the back of the book and tear out ten blank sheets of paper. Then a bunch more. I twist them up tightly, like cigarettes without tobacco. I used to roll my own cigarettes, so I know how much longer the paper will last that way. I tuck them carefully under the grid of branches and twigs. I open the thin box of dry matches. There are only three left. I strike one and it lights the first time. I light the end of the first five twisted pages, then blow on the match end. I quickly turn it around, light the other end, and use it to light the remaining paper twists.

The twigs smoke and smolder. I start to blow and blow underneath them, pushing as much oxygen into the tiny flames as possible. Sparks fly and then the embers glow brightly, but nothing much happens. I start to get nervous, so I pull out a few more sheets of paper and twist them up again, carefully placing them beside the brightest embers. After a few minutes of my blowing, a little fire settles and grows beneath the branches. I lay a few large dry pieces down and then it really picks up. "Yes!" I scream. "Thank you!"

I'm not talking to God. I don't know what or who I'm

talking to. But I start thinking about everyone I've ever loved: my father, whose watch kept me connected to him when I needed him most; my mother's smile and laugh, as rare as it was since my dad died, is still in my heart; my grandmother and all the Christmas mornings before everything ended; even Old Doctor, my foe and friend. Who else?

I look at Paul beside me. His angelic face is sweet and rough all at once. His baby blue eyes. I know no matter what happens, those eyes will always be in my memory and my mind will always hold onto every moment we have spent together. And then I think of Will, a person I've never met but whose words are little vessels of energy traveling across time and space to lance the sickness in my soul.

Now the driest pieces of branch pop with heat and I quickly put an even bigger piece of wood on them. I take a few moments and warm my hands. I've been wearing gloves and have kept my hands from freezing, but the heat coming off the fire stings. I realize how deeply the cold has penetrated into my bones over the past three days.

After a few minutes, I shake Paul gently awake and help him move closer to the fire. He is groggy, but conscious and able to move over. He tries to tell me things, but it is nonsense at this point. I whisper into his ear and tell him to rest. He listens to me and closes his eyes, quickly nodding off again.

I pull the rabbit from the bag, which is now full of blood. I am able to jam one of the sticks under its white fur and skin. After some work, I am able to remove the head and get my fingers beneath the lining of the skin, and with my fingers and the sharp end of the stick, I rip as much of the skin from the body as I can. I take the same stick and jam it through the mouth of the rabbit. Then I hold it over the fire like a child might hold a marshmallow at a campfire. I could never have imagined myself capable of taking a life, never mind dressing and eating it, too. Who am I?

The fire is hot, and the aroma makes my mouth water, and then I imagine what a bear or a wolf might think. My heart sinks, and then I decide that I can't control everything. *Cook the rabbit; eat the rabbit.*

I take the rabbit stick and slide the stick end between two rocks and let the rabbit dangle near the fire. I rub Paul's back and then wrap myself around him to try and keep him warm. I look up to the sky. It is overcast and cloudy. There's a big cold world out there, but I believe this little fire is enough to keep us warm, if only for a few hours.

Chapter 29

I wake alone and near the fire. During the night I rolled away from Paul, who is still sleeping. I can see his chest heaving up and down, so I know he is still alive. It is still dark, and stars fill what's left of the night sky, but there's morning light flowing up over the bottom edges of the horizon.

I am so cold that I feel my body shivering inside and out. I had hoped to wake up a few times during the night to poke the fire and wake Paul, but my exhausted body had other plans. I look at what remains of the fire. A few embers still glow, and I quickly move over and blow on them gently, stoking them until they redden with heat. I rip a large chunk of pages from Will's notebook and rebuild the fire with twigs and small branches until the flames begin to lap at the air.

"What are you doing?"

I turn around and see that Paul has sat up and is staring at me.

"I'm saving the fire—it was dying."

"What's that?" Paul says, pointing at the burnt rabbit I let slow cook all night.

I pick up the stick with the rabbit on the end, and it is charred black and dry as a bone. I grab a leg and tear it off. With my fingers I pull back whatever skin remains and then I bite down. It is heaven. Salty and chewy and heavenly. I take another bite and then another. I'm like a wild animal ripping away the meat.

"How did you get that?" he asks.

"I killed it. I stepped on it and then stabbed it with the stake you made me."

I rip off a leg and hand it to him. He bites into the flesh and then quickly devours it. We quickly tear off the remaining meat and devour what's left of the rabbit. When we are done, we just stare at each other. And then Paul laughs.

"You're a savage, Solis."

"I think I am," I say with a smile. He seems to be more like his old self, like the anger from yesterday dissolved with his fall.

Paul touches his forehead, and dried blood flakes off

onto his jacket. He stares at me, apparently trying to put the pieces together. He is a bit groggy, and his eyes are glassy.

"What happened to me?"

"You fell and hit your head. You broke your arm," I say.

"My chest feels like it was kicked in, too."

He looks at me, and then he points at the fire.

"That's amazing," he says. "How did you start the fire?"

"I used paper from your brother's notebook. I had to. I'm sorry."

Paul's face drops for a moment, and then he puts his head in his good hand. He's thinking about what he should say or do—whether I should be banished or embraced, I imagine. He looks up, and his eyes are blurry and watery. Then he speaks.

"You kept us warm. You made us food that might save our lives. That's more important than a memory."

I nod.

"You read it—I remember you read the letter," he says quietly.

"I'm sorry," I say.

Paul gazes into my eyes. Then he shimmies himself closer to the fire. He winces with each little movement. I pick up his sleeping bag and put it over him and we snuggle together close to the fire. I pull another leg from the rabbit and hand it to his good hand. He bites in and groans from pleasure.

"Will and I lived in the same room together for sixteen years," he starts. "He'd write all kinds of crazy stuff. He was a writer, like my dad. When he died, I think my dad hated me for living. That's crazy-sounding, but I think it's true."

"Yes, they can hate you for living. I know that's true," I say, and I feel the overwhelming truth of it even though I hadn't really thought of it that way before. As much as my mother loves me, she resents that I am here and he is gone. I've never allowed that thought to surface in my conscious-ness before, but there it is, as plain as any truth I know.

He closes his eyes and lays his head down on my lap.

"Will died of cancer, right?"

Paul looks up at me. I see some tears well in his eyes.

"It's okay if you don't want to talk about it."

"Fucking leukemia. I'm sitting around sometimes, waiting for it to grow inside me." He pauses. "It was fast, like six months. One moment we were reading on the beach—well, he was reading, I was probably surfing. And then by winter he was gone."

"I'm sorry," I say. "The faster they go, the harder it is, I think. At least when it takes a long time, you have time to prepare."

Paul reaches out and takes my hand in his. I put my other hand on top of his and then lay my head down gently in his lap.

A cold wind picks up and cuts into us.

"*Fuck*, that's cold," Paul says.

I look up to the mountain before us. It is short, but a steep peak, and I wonder if Paul can even climb it. Snow begins to fall again, and I see that we are in for more rough weather by the clouds that are amassing.

"Can you climb?" I ask.

"Yes. I could climb with no legs and no arms."

"Good."

He sits up all the way and then reaches into his pocket and pulls out the pack of cigarettes he took off the captain.

"Nothing like a smoke after dinner, right?"

"They cause cancer," I say. I'm smiling because I know it's irrelevant—given our situation—but I couldn't help myself.

"My mother would rise from the dead if she saw one of these in my mouth."

"I think we get a survivor's pass at this point, don't you?"

"Yes. 'You can indulge at death's door' is our motto."

We light up and smoke. I inhale deeply and cough a little. Paul just sucks his down.

"I started smoking after she died. I know it makes

no sense, but I wanted to say fuck you to everyone and everything. It drove my brother crazy, and my father would take my packs and throw them away if he found them."

"You do crazy things when people die. It's true."

"Yeah, crazy is the only thing that feels real."

I nod and then inhale. I look up at Paul and then throw the cigarette filter into the fire and lean my head against his shoulder.

After he finishes his smoke, he stands up for the first time since his fall. He winces. He holds the side of his chest and the pain momentarily overwhelms him. He bows and falls to one knee.

"Are you okay?" I ask.

He puts his hand up. He pauses with one knee on the ground for a few moments, gathering his strength. The wind picks up, and it blows frozen snow off the top of drifts. Suddenly, Paul lifts himself and he lets out a loud grunt, his face red and radiating with the effort he's expending to perform this normally simple maneuver.

I hand him the bottle of Tylenol and one of the water bottles. He takes out a handful and drinks the remaining water.

"I'm ready," he says.

We walk to the mountain pass that connects the two peaks. I can see that animal tracks have already made their way to and fro across the pass. It's a good sign. I realize what we were looking at from a distance—what Paul described as a natural bridge—is simply the highest point where the landmasses have remained connected. The animals already knew what we had discovered: to avoid a deadly climb down to the basin of the valley, this was the only place to cross. There's a sheer wall on either side and it's only about ten feet wide, thinner in some places. On top, the pass sits like a thin saddle with very steep drops on either side.

Ice and snow cover it, so Paul and I rope up.

"I'll go first," I say.

He gives me a funny look and says, "World's funny that way."

"Yeah, it doesn't make sense, but I think I'm in charge now, right?"

"I think that's right," he says, nodding for me to go.

I walk out and even though there's ample space on either side, my heart jumps up and down. The ground is slippery and bumpy, and more than once I almost lose my footing. I decide to lie down and crawl across. After about ten feet of crawling, I reach the midpoint, and the trail narrows to only a few feet wide for about a distance of ten feet or so.

I decide to flatten out like a pancake, my arms and

legs straddling around either side of the pass. If I try to crawl across that narrow strip of ice, I fear I'll slip right over the edge.

I slowly shimmy across, careful to move as slowly as I can. I look back a few times at Paul, who is crawling on his hands and knees. I hear him grunting the whole way, and I can only imagine how painful it is when his body slips or slides. Keeping oneself steady on top of the trail requires a constant tightening of the upper-body muscles, the muscle group my gym teacher in middle school called "your core." Paul's core is bruised and perhaps broken. Even a simple trek like what lies before us will be brutally painful for him.

"You have to pancake that part," I yell. I see Paul nod and he tries to lie down in a flat position, but it is too painful. He shakes his head to tell me he can't do it. I put up a hand, telling him to wait.

I shimmy beyond the narrow section of the pass, and then I stand up. I dig my heels into the snow to get as much leverage as I can. Then I triple wrap the rope around my forearms, readying myself. Doubt creeps into my mind for a second, but I push it away. I know I could never hold Paul if he really slipped over the edge, but I can't abandon him.

I nod to Paul to say I'm ready. Paul looks at me and shakes his head.

"You'll never hold me if I fall. It's suicide," he yells. "Sorry—you know what I mean."

"I'm not letting go," I shout back. "You didn't let me go on the cliff."

"That was different—we had a *chance*!"

Then Paul lowers himself onto his belly and he screams, "*Fuck*, this hurts." I know he is doing this for me, so that my life isn't at risk, or at least as much at risk. *Sacrifice*. The word dances in my head, and I can't help but notice how similar *sacrifice* is to *suicide*, but to die for someone else seems so much nobler. Paul begins to shimmy, but it is slow going. I pull the rope gently and work my way backward, offering a little pull with each push he makes with his back legs. Paul screams and hollers with every slide, but he makes his way; and in fifteen minutes or so, he crosses the narrow strip.

We hug each other when he's finally able to stand.

"Thank you," he says.

"What did I do?" I ask, perplexed.

"You were willing to die for me," he says. "Thank you."

I pitch up on my toes and kiss his icy lips. I'm crying. I put a hand on his side as softly as I can and ask if he's okay.

He nods, but his eyes betray the enormity of his pain.

I am filled with hope as I stand at the bottom of the peak.

We climb. It is steep and thickly lined with trees at the bottom, mostly pines. I lead us up the mountain.

It takes the whole morning to ascend the first hundred yards. Our faces are cut and bruised and our necks savaged by the razor-sharp branches. With nearly every step, Paul screams or grunts or swears with pain, mostly from his chest. I call back to him a few times, but he ignores me.

I push my way through a thick clump of trees and there is a break in the tree line.

I'm not sure if it's from the height of the mountain or the lack of water this high up. But I can see the top from where I stand. The climb to the top is clear, studded here and there with trees, rocks, and snow.

"Paul!" I shout.

His glove comes through the bushes first as he pulls himself up above the tree line. His face is white and dull, like the blood is being drained from his body. His legs wobble and he falls to the ground at my feet. I kneel down beside him quickly and, in a flutter of emotion and anxiety, find myself kissing his forehead and hair.

"Paul? Paul?"

He doesn't respond, but his right hand comes around and squeezes me.

"I can't make it, Solis. You should go on."

"Never," I say. "I know it hurts, but you can do it."

He squeezes me again and I squeeze him back and kiss his head again.

"I remember now."

"What?"

"I remember you wanted to die. On the plane."

"Yes, I told you that. But it's not true anymore."

"I don't want to die," he whispers.

"I won't let you. Besides, we have to climb this little mountain."

But we don't go back to climbing right away. He puts his head down in my lap and closes his eyes. Sleep comes quickly and I hold him, trying to be soothing and to provide whatever warmth I can. There's a light snow falling, and the wind has picked up. It's very cold without the trees to protect us. I tell myself I'll let him have fifteen minutes, maybe twenty, but then I'll wake him. We can't get caught here on this mountain if a storm comes.

When I wake, I don't know how long I've been asleep. My heart jumps, and I shake Paul. He's dead asleep, but I'm able to wake him quickly. He startles and then just stares at me, locking on my eyes in the way only he can.

"Did you think I was gone?"

"No," I say quickly, but I look down. I don't want to reveal my fears to him.

"I've got something for you," he says. He opens his bag and pulls out a piece of the candy bar I had handed him the day before. "I saved it in case we needed something extra." He breaks it in half and hands me a piece.

"I can't."

"You can. Open up," he says.

I smile and then kneel down next to him and he slides the piece of chocolate between his teeth. I lean in and kiss him, and bite off half the candy bar.

"That wasn't so bad, was it?"

I shake my head no and smile. I can taste every atom of the chocolate. The salt, sugar, and milk all taste like the very ultimate version of themselves in my mouth.

"We'll have this again, you know," he says.

"Yes. I know we will, but much more."

He stands with a new energy that surprises me.

We begin the ascent and it is clean and purposeful. Paul takes the lead this time, his strength returning like a droopy plant that finds its bloom again in the sun after a long cold night.

It feels like I am floating on the snow. I lean into the mountain, like Paul has told me, and I slam my sticks in at forty-five-degree angles so the snow can hold me. My boots are regular old boots, but the ground is hard, so I'm kicking into the snow trying to create leverage. There are rocks and small bushes to grab and hold. We make better time than I could have hoped and when we reach the top and crest, the whole of the valley is behind us.

I look back once at the darkening valley we just climbed out of. From this view I can see that the nooks and crevices, and the cliffs and overhangs, are flattened into a majestic, romantic vista. Its charms are seductive and had I not just climbed my way out, I would only see the beauty.

While I'm looking at where we've been, Paul looks ahead to where we need to go, and glances up at the heavy cloud cover above us. The snow falls more quickly and the wind up here is brutal and we are completely exposed to all the elements.

But off into the distance, we can both clearly see a path down and off this mountain. We are a day away from the lowlands and, possibly, help.

We look at each other and he pulls me in and says, "Almost home, Solis."

Chapter 30

We walk for a short distance on the top of the mountain. There's a ridge that extends for a while. We find a massive formation of boulders not too far from its edge. They lie in a giant cluster, as if one wave carried them here and dropped them like so many pickup sticks. We walk around until we find a stony lean-to and slide between two of the rocks. It's a natural cave.

Paul rests while I go out in search of any dry wood, but there's nothing up here, plus the snow is wet. We have landed on the moon, I think, except it might be colder.

I find my way back in and Paul has laid out our bags. He has our water bottles out and we have enough melted snow for a few big gulps. My body sucks them in. I can feel the cold water wash down and into my chest and disappear. It's as lovely a taste as anything I've ever had, even if it's cold.

I slide into the bags, but this time Paul faces me. We look into each other's eyes and there's nothing said for what seems like an eternity. What is there to say, really? We have no food. We are alone and lying together at the precipice of what will almost surely be our death. But there is still a possibility for rescue and salvation. It could be a moment away, but then again, so could death.

His left hand is flat against the small of my back and he pulls me in tightly and kisses me on the lips. Both our lips are hard and chapped, but somehow, the kiss is softer than anything I've ever felt before. I kiss him back, first on the lips, then his cheek and neck.

His hand is cold and I can feel it on my body, moving and caressing along the lines, often touching and pushing beyond what I expect, but toward what I want.

I touch him too, and we explore each other as fully as we can with the cold and his damages. We softly whisper our hesitation and our approval, perfectly attuned to each other. He turns me to my back and presses his full body against mine. He kisses me, and I forget the world. The past. The future. Our pain and suffering. Everything disappears for what seems like forever in a kind of indescribable bliss.

● ● ●

We wake together to the sound of wind howling and flakes drifting into our lean-to: evidence of a storm rolling in.

"Hey," he says, kissing my lips.

"Hey," I say.

"Solis?"

"Yes," I say.

"When the storm blows over, you have to leave me."

I prop myself on one elbow in surprise.

"Don't be ridiculous."

"You have to. I'm dying. If you don't go, I'll definitely die here and I'd rather not die here."

The world giveth and the world taketh away. This is why I hate the world. I close my eyes and see my father putting tinsel on our Christmas tree. My stocking is hung beside his and Mom's. There are candy canes everywhere. He's doing a manic dance around the tree, singing, "Here comes Santa Claus, here comes Santa Claus." He hands me a gift. "A little something early, darling." And then he disappears into the kitchen and eventually into the bedroom, where later that night, he will blow his head off. I still have the gift. It was a portrait he did of me in a little white dress with yellow and pink hearts sewn on. My mother made that dress. I've kept the portrait, contrary to what I've told Old Doctor. And sometimes I pull it out and cry, like I am right now just thinking about it. But I'd be lying if I said the thought of it hasn't brought me some joy, too.

He takes hold of my hand and moves it down to where his ribs are broken and I feel the swelling and the heat rising off his chest.

"I'm bleeding inside," he says. "I feel it. My heart feels weak."

A gasping sob comes from nowhere and I put my head on his chest. And I cry harder and harder, and he holds me, stroking my hair.

I kiss him on the neck a few times, then look into his eyes. Nobody has ever said those words to me before. I don't know how to speak for a moment, and then a huge lump lodges in my throat.

"What can I do?" I cry.

"Nothing right now. But when the storm stops, leave me."

There's a long pause, and I'm trying to process all the emotions I'm feeling. It's overwhelming, but I decide on a simple idea.

"I'll find help."

He nods, but it doesn't mean yes, find me help. It means say whatever you have to say in order to go away and feel okay about it. Lie if we must, but you can carry on for the two of us.

"Read to me," he says, after a long silence. "The letter."
I can see the dark rings circling his eyes now. I look at his skin more closely and even in the darkness his pale skin glows yellow.

I pull the letter from my pocket and begin to read.

I feel a soft sob pulse through Paul's body and I stop reading and listen.

"Are you okay? Is it too much?"

"No, it's good. I miss him."

"I'm sorry."

"He died a day or two before I was sixteen. It is sweet, somehow, to hear your voice layering over his."

"Should I keep going? "

"Yes."

I put my hand through his hair and kiss his cheek. I return to the beginning, and I read to him. And then I read it again, and tears stream down his face.

When I finish, Paul reaches up and pulls me into him and kisses me.

"Can you tear me a piece of paper from the diary and get me the pen from my backpack?"

I reach over and grab his backpack and find a pen. I tear a sheet and hand him the book. He scribbles down something quickly and folds it up.

"Give this to my father when you get down," he tells me.

"You'll give it to him, okay?" My voice is choked with tears.

He puts his hand on my face as tears roll down. Cold air swirls around us.

We kiss again and again. Then I open the paper and look at the note. It is so simple it breaks my heart into two:

Dad,
I love you. I'm sorry.
             Paul

Chapter 31

I wake first and morbidly put my hand on Paul's chest to make sure he is alive. His heart still beats and I can hear his breathing, though it sounds wheezy and shallow. The long rest has rejuvenated my body a bit, and I feel strong and determined, if also stiff and cold. I will find help for Paul or die trying.

While he sleeps, I pack up my sleeping bag and my bottle. I grab the hiking sticks, though I hope I won't need them.

When I'm ready, I shake Paul and he reaches with his hand and holds mine.

"Come back for me. Even if it is long after I'm dead. Promise you'll come back here."

"Stop it. I'll bring back someone who will help you. You'll be alive when I come back."

My voice chokes on the word *alive*. I'm looking at his body, and I can see how cold and pale and beaten he is. My hope is draining moment by moment, like the blood in his body. I feel helpless and angry, but I buck up and show him that I'm not afraid for myself or for him and that I'll be back.

"It's okay," he says. "Maybe fate has plans."

"Do you believe that?"

"I believe we found each other."

"Like we were meant to."

He nods.

"Before my mother died, she told me she'd be a star in the night and I could always look up and find her. I believed that for a long time."

"That's so sweet," I tell him.

"If you need me," he says, lying back as if he lacks the strength to stay upright.

"Okay," I tell him, "you too. If you need me."

I kiss him one more time as deeply and lovingly as my dry lips and bereft heart can muster. He cradles my cheek against his. Then he kisses me one more time on my eyes and whispers, "Goodbye."

A short cry bursts from my chest, and I feel his chest heave, and we hold onto each other for just a moment longer. Then I turn and walk.

"I love you, Jane," he calls out.

I stop walking and turn around. I take him in deeply with my eyes so my heart and brain never forget this moment or this beautiful boy who will always be mine. "I love you too," I cry out. I bring a big mitten to my mouth and blow him a kiss. He smiles his big, crooked, awkward, lovely smile. I will never forget that.

I walk away from our shelter. He is alone with his brother's words, the memory of my kiss, and the fear that this is the end of his time on earth. *I will find help.*

I walk along the ridge, and it's like walking through clouds. The mountain fog rolls around me, and it is impossible to know where I'm headed. Paul directed me to walk straight on the ridge, and from the daylight before the last storm, it appeared to descend and flatten out near here. If I can get to ground level, in an open space, and if the snow and cloud banks clear, I'm certain I'll be found by a plane or somebody searching for us.

It's a lot of ifs.

The ridge quickly flattens out and then descends into a steep, long slope that isn't nearly as rocky as the valley. The tree line comes into view, and I am grateful for its protection from the wind. I often look up in the sky, hoping to see a plane. At one point I hear a faraway something, and I allow myself to imagine an airplane that will find me and then swoop in to save Paul. I push out all thoughts of him lying there alone and simply replay our night together, over and over.

By early afternoon, my legs shake and wobble. Each step requires strength my body no longer has. I fight to focus on moving and just keep Paul's name as my mantra. If searchers were to find me now, they'd think I was a homeless person mumbling some psychotic chant about a long-lost relative. But it is the chanting, the repetition of just his name, that keeps me going.

By late afternoon I've reached the bottom, and I look out across a long stretch of flat terrain. It is open, and my mind tells me it is where I'll be found. My gut checks me, though. Shelter. I can hear Paul's voice saying that after water, shelter is everything. The trees and rocks offer me shelter and my best chance of survival if the weather turns, but the open grassland offers the greatest chance of being found and Paul being saved.

My first step into the open grass is deep and I realize the snow here accumulates in a way that isn't true of the mountain slope protected by trees. Nor is it cold enough to create hardened snow, like on the top of the mountain. It isn't a warning, I tell myself as I take another step and then another. It is the hardest walking I've done since this journey began. My legs are so tired it requires every ounce of energy to pull my feet free from the snow. The farther out I get, the deeper the drifts become, and I find myself becoming frustrated by my progress as night falls quickly around me.

The wind picks up and is vicious like never before. With each gust, I feel the temperature dropping. Here I am again. One way or another, I keep reliving that moment on the plane with the pills in my hand. I'm never going to make it across, and the cold is so severe I simply won't survive the night.

I stop and turn my back to the wind and look back toward Paul. *I'm sorry,* I think. A tear freezes right on my cheek and I imagine his face before me. Words come and connect us. *The snow is your friend,* I hear him say. I don't recall that he ever said that to me before, but the word *snow* reverberates throughout my head and heart. I start to dig and dig until I hit the earth. It is perhaps three feet deep. I work my way back toward Paul, digging out a grave the length of my body. I unfold my sleeping bag and stand in it. I zip the bag up to my armpits and sit in my snow grave.

I quickly shovel snow onto my feet and my legs and eventually cover my chest. I zip up my bag all the way and use my right hand to pull as much snow over me as possible. I pull my hand in and listen and feel for my fate. The wind is gone, or at least its chill does not touch me in the same way here. The bag is keeping my heat inside, and the cold from the snow is not enough to penetrate, at least not yet.

I smile as I hear Paul say, *Solis, well done*. I close my eyes and, just before I fall off, I have one thought: *He spoke to me. It wasn't memory.*

Chapter 32

Another night without dreams. Dead. Soundless. I wake before dawn and hear nothing. No howling. No wind. I am warm, but the chill of the snow is there, and I immediately claw my way out and stand up.

"I'm alive," I shout. "Paul, wherever you are, I'm alive."

I roll up my bag and drink the small amount of water that melted in my overnight bottle. My legs have not recovered, and I can feel the pain and ache in them from the very first step.

I push across the open grass and the farther I go, the more endless it seems. I fear my mind is slipping as I keep looking around, feeling that somebody is following me. For a minute I imagine it is Paul, who recovered and decided to come find and save me. But he never comes.

You can dream all you want, Jane, I tell myself, *but this is just about you. Focus, Solis, focus.*

I near the wooded forest on the horizon. I've trudged for most of the day in knee- and thigh-deep snow. My legs are dead and frozen in a way they've never been. I look back and there's a sight so horrific, I gag.

It isn't Paul that's been following me, but a wolf. A lone black wolf, moving sideways and forward. I watch it zigzag along, and at first I think it might be hunting for rabbits or prairie dogs. But now I feel its eyes on me; it's walking slowly, stalking me, waiting for me to falter. Then it will pounce on me and rip the meat from my bones.

With each step, I see the wolf coming closer. The closer the wooded area is, the nearer the wolf comes to me. Does he know that safety might lie just beyond the flat snow grasses for me? I experience a burst of adrenaline and move through the final twenty yards of snow and grass faster than I would have thought possible.

I glance behind me often. As my pace increases, so does the wolf's. He trots and seems to be following a straighter path than before. He pauses when I look directly at him. I sense there is some fear in him as well. The thought of that emboldens me. *The big bad wolf is afraid of me!* Well, maybe not afraid, but he's being cautious before he launches an attack.

I reach the wooded area and turn quickly, sizing up the wolf. He is bone thin. He stops in his tracks, and for the first time, he doesn't turn his head. I want to run, but something in my gut tells me to stand still, if even for a second. His eyes are yellow and his fur is mostly black with grayish patches. He leans awkwardly on his left paw, lifting his right. *Is he injured?* I can't tell. I've yet to see any other wolves. *Has he left his pack or been left behind?*

With his probable injury, I suspect his speed is limited and his limited ability to climb is further diminished. I reach a large pine tree about fifty feet into the woods and begin climbing it. I stop for a moment to look back, but I don't see anything. *If he had wanted to attack me straight on, it would have happened already, right? Just climb, Jane, climb.*

The tree is thick with branches and each snow-encrusted branch takes a minute to navigate, but I make steady progress up the trunk. I think I hear a soft growl below me, but I do not look down. Then there's some scratching on the trunk, but I convince myself that his injury will prevent him from climbing. And even if he can climb, I'd rather fight him from above in a tree then in an open field, where he would surely overpower me.

I slip and slide my way a good twenty feet up, find a good perch, and stop. I pull out my two climbing sticks and sit and wait to do battle. I'll probably die up here, but at least I'll die fighting. Is that a little bloodlust moving through my veins? I almost relish a fight at this point. I sense an uninhibited craziness brewing inside me, but it's so different from what I felt at the hospital. It has purpose, and I'm in control of it.

I wait and listen but hear nothing except the normal night sounds of the forest. The wind whistles softly, a branch breaks and falls in the distance, and I listen to the rustling of trees against one another. A little fear snakes up my back as I imagine the wolf making its way up the branches, slinking slowly and methodically.

Would I hear it? In this darkness, will I hear it climb? I push the thoughts from my head. *Don't let the voices take over again, Jane.* I think of Paul, and I wonder if he's alive. The wind blows and I imagine that's him sending me a hug from afar.

But what am I going to do? I can't go down now.

I unroll my sleeping bag and perch on a clump of large branches, hooking my feet under and over them to brace myself. I snuggle down into the bag, zip and seal the top, and press my back against the trunk as firmly as possible.

As I sit in this tree, I contemplate the cold. I am freezing now beyond comprehension. I know that the temperature outside is mild compared to what we faced before, so the chill in my bones frightens me. I'm cold now because my body is running out of energy, and it's damaged by my exertion and exposure for the last few days. I may be stronger than I thought I was, but I'm weakening too. I can only hope that somebody finds me soon.

Chapter 33

I'm awake all night. Adrenaline is pumping through my body, which has gone into a serious protection mode, with all my sensory powers on full alert. I register every twig snap from miles away, and I find myself twitching constantly until the sun rises.

From up in the tree, I watch dawn begin to spread across the sky. It is clear, and I think it will be warm. *This is it*, I promise myself. *This is my day. This is the day I walk out of here. This is the day I find help for Paul.*

I climb down slowly and have my sticks at the ready. When I touch ground, I look around carefully and see that there are paw prints all around the tree but no sign of the wolf. I start to walk west, resuming the direction I've been traveling.

It is slow going. The forest is thick, hilly, and full of rocks, large and small. I'm tired and my nerves are shot from last night, so I trip and fall more than usual. Each time I fall, I panic and anticipate the wolf. My knees buckle several times as my legs weaken from the stress and lack of nourishment. My body, which has been working harder than I ever asked it to before, craves water more than anything else. It is the first time I fear dehydration, but if I choose to eat the snow, hypothermia will kill me. Despite its early promise, the sun disappears behind a cloud bank. I shake my head at my earlier optimism. But I don't feel pathetic or disgusted the way I might have last week. It's better than having no sun at all. I celebrate its warmth even as I feel disappointment. I've just got to hang on until the clouds move by again. I keep moving, one foot in front of the other.

My hands are starting to freeze. They've been cold for days, but this morning I notice how numb the fingers on my left hand feel. I look at the tips of my fingers, and they look darker. I can't decide if it's paranoia; I'm pretty sure it's real, but I'm not sure if it means I'll lose my fingers.

My mind flashes on the knife in my hand and the time not so long ago when I thought slicing myself would bring me some kind of joy. Now the thought of losing even an ounce of my blood repulses me. I wiggle my fingers for a second and pray that I can keep them in the end.

At around noon, I stop walking. I've been fighting for hours, and I don't feel like I've made much progress. I find a large stick and pick it up. It's about six inches taller than my head, fits nicely in my hands, and feels sturdy. I walk with it, and it provides the balance and support that I desperately need. I only wish I'd stumbled on the idea earlier.

When I first hear the sound of the river, it comes as a dull roar. At first there is a low tone, like the moan of tired television in a distant room. But it grows louder with each step I take, and eventually the correct synapses in my brain fire and connect, and I get it. River. Water. I pick up my pace and quickly find myself standing on top of a ravine, looking down at a thick, lush, flowing river.

I look north and south, up and down the river, but there's no entry point. I could try to walk along the river, but I'm not entirely sure my body can carry me any farther. With water, yes, I could keep going. But between the lack of food and dehydration, I'm dead on my feet. It's so close. I look down. The drop is maybe fifteen feet down a sloping hill that would take me to the river's edge. I try to calculate how damaging the fall will be, factoring in the snow and the slope, but in the end, it is less complicated than the algebra exams I always failed. If I try to walk the edge of the ravine, I will definitely die. If I jump, I'll probably die. I weigh my options and opt for probably die.

I walk a few yards in each direction, looking for the ideal place to jump. I know from gym class I'm supposed to bend my knees when I land and roll forward. I toss my stick down and it hits the ground and rolls toward the riverbank. It doesn't snap or break. It bounces and tumbles a bit, but it survives intact. I'll be able to use it to walk with me another mile or two.

I'm going to count to three and then leap. *God, please help me*, I think. One. *Paul, stay with me.* Two. *Paul, I'm coming back for you.* Three. *Jump, Jane, jump.* I leap and for a long, sick second, I hover in the air before my body yields to the force of gravity. The downward rush takes over and I just fall until—*bang!*—my feet hit the ground hard. Although my legs are bent and some of the fall is absorbed by my thighs and calves, it still jolts my body like a lightning bolt. I pitch forward through air, banging my face into the snow, then flipping again, landing on my feet momentarily and finally collapsing as my ankles give way and I roll over. I roll and tumble until I hit the riverbank.

Finally, I stop rolling and lie there panting, on my back, afraid to move. I open my eyes and watch the gloomy, gray clouds low in the sky.

I'm alive, I say quietly to no one. Or maybe I just think

it; I'm not sure. My wrists and hands are, amazingly, un-
hurt, but my left ankle swells immediately and the pain is
enormous. I can bend it a bit, so I know it isn't broken. I
try my best with my frozen hands to tighten the boot. The
loud roar of the river fills my ears and suddenly the cot-
ton feeling of my mouth blooms into my consciousness
and crowds out any other thoughts. I get on all fours and
crawl the rest of the way to the river. The water moves very
quickly, and I'm careful not to lean too far in for fear of
getting swept away. That's a headline I'd rather not imagine: GIRL HIKES OUT OF VALLEY ONLY TO FALL INTO RIVER.

I get to the edge of the river and gulp down the water.
Food. Drink. Candy. Rabbit. You name it. Nothing has
ever tasted as deeply refreshing as the river water. The
thick, icy water splashes into my mouth with such force
that I nearly choke on it. I try to keep as dry as I can, but
water flows down my throat and spills into my jacket and
onto my chest and stomach. I pull back for a few seconds
before I lap up some more. I repeat this scenario until my
stomach swells, and I simply roll onto my back and pass
out.

When I wake, I am still thirsty, but a few more pulls off
the river soothe me. My stomach is in knots, though. I feel
the full effort of the day in my bones, and the hell of the
journey still ahead of me looms. A single sit-up is needed,

but the energy and desire have dissipated. *Rest, then try. Rest, then try.*

I close my eyes, and my mind drifts until my father appears. He's young, like in the photo on my mother's dresser. He's wearing a white sweater with dark blue-and-red trim around a small V-neck, the same one he wore on his last Christmas Eve. He's very tan and wearing sunglasses that hide his sad eyes.

"I'm okay," he says.

I reach out to touch him. His face is smooth, and the smell of Old Spice lingers in the air. I move his face to the side so I can look at his profile, but what I really want to see is the hole in his head. It's black and scabbed over with dark, wine-colored blood. I place my fingertips over the hole, and I dig in gently and remove a silver bullet and blood starts to flow down his cheek.

He turns back and puts his warm hand on my face. *"Thank you, Jane. I'm okay. Go ahead without me. I'm okay."*

I nod and I start to cry, his hand wiping each tear away.

"I'm okay too, Daddy."

And I believe it, too. That's the first time I've ever felt that way, dream or no dream, since the day my father killed himself. The blackness swirling through my mind begins to echo with the sound of the shot, my mother's screams, and the noise of sirens and walkie-talkies, medics and policemen. My father died that night, but something inside of me started to grow, and at first, I tended it, helping it, but then I lost control and it grew into something that existed all on its own: a raging beast inside of me that almost devoured me from the inside out.

"Goodbye," I tell my father, and I touch his face once more and he leans into me, very close. I can feel the imprint of his kiss. Then his face turns mean and ugly and I can feel his breath on the top of my nose.

I open my eyes, and for a split second I am looking up into the yellow eyes of the wolf. Then suddenly, *snap!* The icy wind hits my face and I awake.

I'm frozen and panting from my dream.

I stand up and grab my walking stick and look upriver and then down. There's no sign of the wolf. *It was just a dream, Jane. The wolf is only as real as your father. Let them go.*

I turn and head downriver with the wind at my back. Walking the riverbank is the easiest walk I've had since I started. That's good, because my body is failing me now, and every hundred feet or so, I have to kneel down and gather my strength. Eventually, with the help of the wind pushing me forward, I feel some energy. I'm thinking about that last climb Paul made and how he came to life on that day, just before he took a turn for the worse.

Is he still alive? How could he be? He just has to be. Don't give up on him. My thoughts turn to the people who never gave up on me. My mother, Old Doctor, the nurses, some of the other Life Housers like Ben. I remember one day in the hospital; it was a low point perhaps a couple months into my stay. I was looking out at the courtyard filled with snow. I was thinking about how wonderful snow is to a child. Sledding, snowmen, snowball fights. And it must have made me sad, because tears were rolling down my face and Ben came up to me and sat down. He didn't say much, but he offered me a cigarette. And even though I wasn't a smoker, I joined him out in the court-yard. When we were done, he said, "Everything I look at has the potential to make me sad."

"I love the snow," I said. "But it makes me sad."

"Yeah. It makes me sad too," Ben said.

"It makes me miss my father. We played in the snow—I still think about that a lot."

Then he did something that made my mouth drop but I now realize was perhaps the grandest gesture ever committed at Life House. He pulled down his pants and took a pee in the pristine white snow, spelling his name.

"Now you'll think of me."

I laughed. And it makes me smile even now.

My pace steadies, and I move along the river until it takes a wide turn back toward the mountain range I left days before. It is so easy to walk along the river and follow its path mindlessly. But I feel the sun, and I know where that river is going. I can't go back there. I stop and look across the river, considering my options. As far as I can see from here, there's nothing but an open field of grass beyond the underbrush. Cross and take my chances of dying from exposure in the middle of the field? Or follow a river back toward a world I know holds certain death for me?

My eyes focus deep into the vast expanse beyond the river and follow a clear dark line straight along the horizon. Is that a fence? A road? A power line? A logging road? It must be man-made, whatever it is. Nothing in nature could cut such a long, straight line across the horizon. It occurs to me that my eyes could be playing tricks on me.

The first thing standing between the line on the horizon and me is a narrow piece of river. I step to the edge of the riverbank and look down to where the bend breaks. It is probably fifteen or twenty feet across at the narrowest point, maybe less. The river isn't deep; I can tell because I can see it rippling off the rocks on the bottom.

I take out all my dry clothes: a pair of pants, a shirt and sweater, two pairs of wool socks, and my jacket and shell, and I put them into a plastic bag and tie it. Then I put the bag in my sleeping bag, knowing I must keep my clothes dry if I am to survive crossing the river.

I shimmy down the bank and slide into the water with both boots. The slow-moving current is more powerful than I anticipated, but it only goes up to my shins. I plant my full weight and hold the bank with my arms so as not to be swept away. I look up to the bank and know that scrambling back up isn't an option. I take a deep breath. *Let me cross. Let me cross.*

Chapter 34

I stand still for a moment, taking in the strength of the current and the distance I have to cover. *It is less than twenty feet,* I tell myself. *You can do this.* I walk out and the current stays around knee level for the first two or three steps, then the water is up to my thighs and its chill is bracing.

I jam my stick as far out as I can manage but am pushed a few feet downstream as I do it. I step and push against the stick like a pole vault jumper, and the current sweeps me up. I flutter kick as fast as I can and push hard against the stick and I'm able to move two or three yards across the river. *Don't fight it, Jane. Let the river move you.* I try pulling my stick back toward me, but the force of the drag makes it impossible. I see it float away, rushing in the current, and I feel like I'm losing my best friend.

I'm moving quickly and making progress, but the bend is closer than I expected. I don't fight the current; it floats me directly toward the far bank. The cold of the water strangles my muscles, and I am struggling to stay afloat. Their tightness makes lifting my arm from the water nearly impossible. My body feels heavy and numb. For a moment, my head is swallowed by the heavy drag from below. I get my mouth just above the waterline and gasp, trying to inhale deeply. My lungs feel frozen.

My legs are numb and weighted down by my waterlogged pants and heavy boots. My treading slows, then stops. I flail my arms, but the cold has numbed my shoulders. I look up, and I can see that I'm halfway across but stuck in the center sweep of the current. When the river breaks right, I need to be near the bank so I can stop my forward momentum. But I have nothing left. The fight in my legs is gone, and my arms offer no more force than a feather against the churning, moving beast.

Just as I hit the bend, the river roils and my feet graze the rocky bottom. I immediately kick back and run through the mud, and the effort ignites my arms, which thrash into the water with ferocity. My body lurches toward the shoreline, and I slam into the riverbank just before it turns sharply and cups the excess roiling water.

I drag myself up, drape myself over the lip of the bank,

and hook my right leg over the top, rolling myself onto solid ground. I cough and heave water and bile into the snow. I am shaking and sobbing and my fingers and hands begin to burn with pain. After a while, I get on my knees to fling off my sleeping bag. I have no idea how much or how little time has passed. I push my frozen arms into the frozen bag and grab the ties with my teeth. I pull the knot free, and the bag unrolls.

I put my knee on the lip of the sleeping bag, but I can't hold the edge of the lining with my frozen fingers, so I bite the corner and pull it open with my teeth. I reach in and grab my clothes. My hands are about as useful as clubs, but I manage. The bag is damp, but my clothes are dry.

I'm clumsy, but I get my clothes and jacket on and keep my frozen hands close to my heart underneath my clothes. They'll never warm up under these conditions, but my hope is to stave off hypothermia as long as possible. I drape the wet sleeping bag over my body, propping the top shielded corner over my head. From a distance I must look like a sheik or nomad with a long, dark green cape, tromping over the snow.

I can see the dark line in the distance. I look to the sky and suddenly, for the first time since the crash, the sun comes out in full force. It warms my face.

I have to cross this field before the sun falls. A night

under the snow—under a wet sleeping bag with soaking pants—will find me gone by morning.

My body shakes with chills. Early on, the exercise created warmth, and I could capture that heat to melt water or warm my hands or, with Paul, to heat our bodies at night. But I'm no longer able to generate heat. I may make the horizon, but if nobody is there to help me, I'll be dead by dawn.

Chapter 35

I walk, and the sun sets around me. There's a low ceiling of dark clouds circling me. Snow is falling—at first lightly, but then the heavier stuff moves in and the wind starts to pick up. Luckily the wind remains at my back. I focus my mind on one thing I know is true: behind the clouds, the sun was as bright today as it has ever been. Clouds come and go, so do storms and rain and wind, but the sun will rise every morning.

I imagine it rising backward, breaking through the clouds, warming me and drying my clothes. I imagine its light pouring across the river, making it sparkle, and filtering over the valley and the mountains, making them glow. I imagine Paul standing up on the mountain, bathing himself in the warmth of the sun. I smile at the thought, and I imagine feeling the warmth of his body against mine and see us standing together in sun. He is whispering my name over and over, "Jane, Jane, Jane."

A tear wells up in my eye and I feel its warmth roll slowly down my face, and then another falls. I don't why I'm crying, but I know somewhere inside I'm melting. The long path I've walked since crashing into that mountain has brought me to this moment. Old Doctor would say that I've been on this journey for a lot longer than my six days in this frozen apocalypse. A week ago, if I were in session with him or the group, I would have snickered, probably to myself, about what a load of crap it all was. But today, I can see the long arc on which I've been walking.

Before I reach the thick black line against the horizon, I actually come to a barbed wire fence. I lay the sleeping bag over the wire and just flop over it. I have no strength or agility left to be cautious, and a sharp wire hooks into my left forearm, ripping a long gash from elbow to my thumb. The stuffing pours out of my jacket, and the material turns dark as it soaks up the blood. I try for a moment to untangle the sleeping bag from the wire, but it is completely enmeshed. With every tug, it tears.

This is it, I think, *no bag tonight. I've got to beat the dark.* I trudge forward. The snow is in deep drifts and the ground is uneven. Each step is unsteady, and my mind swirls with memories and fantasies and the two become one. Suddenly, a future appears, and Paul is holding me beside a Christmas tree. There are stockings and gifts, and on the table behind us there are photos of the dead: my father; Paul's brother, Will; and the photo of Old Doctor and his dad on the fishing boat. Old Doctor is there himself, talking with my mother, and I can see smiles on their faces. He just keeps nodding and grinning as my mother tells him something I can't hear. Then he winks at me and mouths, "You're okay, Jane." I nod at him and put my hand around Paul's back.

I look up and there's a light shining in the distance. It is so far away, but I can feel its warmth on my face, as if it were the sun itself. I stumble and fall and see a smear of blood against the snow. *Get up, Jane.*

I stand, and a big gust of wind hits my back and the snow swirls before my eyes. I focus on the light before me. *One step at a time,* I think. *Walk toward that light.* I look up and it can't be too far, no farther than a city block or two, but no matter how many steps I take, it still feels far away.

I stumble again, and this time I fall face-first into the snow, and my head hits a patch of ice. The knock is hard enough to make my ears ring, but I don't black out. My chest heaves up and down, trying to draw in oxygen. No matter how much I take in, I can't seem to catch my breath.

I can't believe I've come this close, but my legs won't move. I'm dizzy and buzzing with excitement. Just then, I feel somebody lift me from my right side, and I turn to find myself leaning into Paul, who is carrying me. He whispers into my ear, but I can't understand him.

I'm unable to speak, I'm so happy to see and feel him. He looks fine; he looks amazing. It doesn't seem right, and yet it's so perfect and I'm so grateful to see him that it doesn't matter that I don't understand what's happening. I'm looking at him, not in front of me—which is how I find myself walking directly into a fence that separates me from the dark strip of road and the heavy, warm light on the opposite side. I fall to my knees and for a moment I think Paul's gone, and I fear I can't rise. I just can't move anymore. I lie in the snow and listen to my shallow breathing.

But then Paul is here again. He reaches down and picks me up under both shoulders. He whispers—a nothingness, but it is pure love in my mind.

He keeps an arm around my shoulders, and I hold his waist as we trudge our way to the road. I hear voices, both familiar and far away. I touch his hair, his face, his lips. He stops walking.

And then he disappears, leaving me on the side of the

road. I hear nothing but the sound of my own labored breath. The clouds have cleared, and I can see stars shining at me in a clear night sky. I scan them dumbly and watch one star sparkle and glow, holding my eye until I lose it or it dissolves into the blackness, I'm not sure which.

Epilogue

6 Months Later

I never returned to Life House Institute after I walked off the mountain.

I remember waking up in a hospital room. It was as if I had never left Life House. Antiseptic air and dull light filled my room. Was it real? The crash, Paul, the long walk, the wolf, the light . . . I didn't know. I searched my memory until my head hurt, literally. The plane and the pills and even my obsession with the Plan flooded back to me. Had I actually followed through with the Plan and swallowed the pills? Could this be heaven? Hell?

And then I heard a familiar sound. It was the sound of a throat clearing, discreetly. I looked up to see Old Doctor sitting in a chair in the corner of the room, waiting for me. His sad eyes crinkled as he smiled at me.

"Hey," I said.

"Jane. I'm so happy to hear your voice again."

I started to cry.

"I'm happy too," I whispered.

"Your mother is on her way from New Jersey," he said. He walked over and put his hand over mine, weighted with all the care in the world. His skin was soft and warm.

"You're okay, Jane. Your mother will be here soon."

I looked down at my left hand to find it bruised and swollen. My palms were raw and red. I examined the rest of my body and found it intact. I wiggled my feet and scrunched my toes. All there.

"Where am I?" I asked.

He stood and moved closer to me. He studied my face, and I think he might have been holding back some emotion of his own.

"It's over now," he told me. "You're back in the world, Jane."

• • •

I've spoken to so many people since I walked out of those mountains. Doctors, rangers, reporters, hikers, climbers, survivalists, my family, friends of my family. They all want to know how I survived. I wish I knew the answer, but I really don't. I have developed a pat response, where I draw an analogy to having a gun pointed at my head:

move or die. I moved and I chose living. Everyone likes this idea.

The night I was found, a truck driver named William Roberts slowed his truck to a stop and hit the floodlight mounted on the roof of his truck. It was a cold and snowy night. He was seventeen miles from the main road but stopped because something weird caught his eye. He grabbed a pistol from his glove compartment and stepped out of his truck, walking slowly over to my nearly life-less body. He said he didn't know if maybe he might have to shoot an animal if it were suffering. Or he thought it might be some kind of strange trick. He looked around, wondering if maybe someone was hiding in the brush.

He knelt down next to me and put his hand over my mouth. Faint, warm air moistened his fingers. *Whoever she is, she's still alive,* he thought. And then he picked up my body and carried me to his truck. He laid me down in the front seat, releasing the back of the passenger seat so it lay relatively flat. He turned his truck around and drove back toward town.

He told the press that I never woke the whole time we drove. He took me past town, which was seventy-five miles from where he found me, and then straight to the hospital that was fifty miles farther south. If he hadn't done it, I'd be dead right now. But he did it. And when they got me into the hospital, they pumped me full of drugs and warm water, slowly bringing my body temperature back up.

Mr. Roberts waited to see if I would live. He sat in the hospital waiting room until a doctor returned to confirm that I was going to survive. He got in his truck and drove back home. Later that week, reporters tracked him down and asked why he didn't wait for the reward. My mother had offered a small reward to anyone stupid enough to travel up into the mountains to find me during the storm, and there'd been no takers. He said he was just doing what anybody else would have done. It doesn't amaze me anymore after what Paul and I did for each other, but it is still heartening to know that the world is filled with good souls.

The deep cold made it difficult for the doctors to determine the time of Paul's death with any accuracy. The coroner's report said he died a day or two after I left him on the mountain. I believe I know the exact timing of his death, but that is a secret I intend to keep to myself.

A few months after I left the hospital, I received a small package posted from Cambridge, Mass. It was wrapped in brown paper, and the return address was marked in large block letters: FROM WILL HART SR. I felt the hairs rise on my neck. I picked up the package and carefully unsealed the edges and slid the box out of the paper. I wanted to preserve the package—to save anything with a connection to Paul.

I opened the box. Inside, wrapped in a monogrammed handkerchief, was Will's book. A note card was tucked inside, intentionally placed sideways with its edge sticking out, so as not to be missed.

I removed the note.

Dear Jane,

I've wanted to write to you for some time now. Thank you for sending his short, sweet note. It means the world to me. Also, I've had time to digest your account of your amazing story. I know my son and everything you say rings true. He was always a brave boy. As you may know, they found a book in his hand. I opened the book and realized the only thing written in it was addressed to you. I read it; I'm sure you will forgive me such a trespass. Because of its nature, and his obvious desire for you to read it, I'm returning this book to you.

Yours,
Will Hart, Sr.

I opened the box and carefully unwrapped the hand-kerchief, fingering the *PH* monogrammed in the bottom-right-hand corner of the cloth. I flipped open the cover and my fingertips traced Will's name, carved into the leather. And then I turned over the first pages, and there on the very next page was a note scrawled in block letters, clearly written by a frozen hand.

> Jane,
> I'm so cold and tired and hungry. I can't think.
> I'm so sorry. You'll survive. Everything. Pills, razors,
> heartbreak, me, your dad, your mom, doctors,
> bad thoughts, this dumb fucking mountain.
> Don't quit. Fight, crawl, scratch, scream, punch.
> Just hold on, keep breathing through it all. Walk
> off this mountain. Live for us. You're strong and
> awesome and amazing and a million other words
> I can't think of right now.
>
>   I love you.
>   P

I read Paul's letter again, and even now, after dozens of times, a big fat tear wells and hovers in my eye. Then it rolls down my cheek and falls on the page, splashing the dry paper, sealing our emotions together forever.

I open my window and look up at the stars. There are millions out there shining away. I know they are not lost souls or anything like that. In the physical world, they are merely suns like our own: burning balls of fire that heat the universe. But I believe Paul is out there somewhere.

If Old Doctor asked me to explain how I survived up there, I would simply say, "With love and luck." Where is our love now? On the pages of this book, in the crevices of my brain, in a bright star a couple billion miles away. And when I die—which I hope won't be for a long time—that love will remain.

I close my eyes and look into the night at one of dozens of twinkling stars. I feel Paul with me, saying my name, whispering and laughing. I grip the book and lay it across my chest. I hear the trees dancing in the wind and the sound of insects calling. And we are here, Paul and me—separated but connected, brokenhearted but grateful.

I open my window to the night and let my left arm hang over the sill. A cool stream of air wafts by, and my fingertips tingle as the night breeze flows over and through them. I smile, knowing how lucky I am to be alive.

EGMONT PRESS: ETHICAL PUBLISHING

Egmont Press is about turning writers into successful authors and children into passionate readers – producing books that enrich and entertain. As a responsible children's publisher, we go even further, considering the world in which our consumers are growing up.

Safety First
Naturally, all of our books meet legal safety requirements. But we go further than this; every book with play value is tested to the highest standards – if it fails, it's back to the drawing-board.

Made Fairly
We are working to ensure that the workers involved in our supply chain – the people that make our books – are treated with fairness and respect.

Responsible Forestry
We are committed to ensuring all our papers come from environmentally and socially responsible forest sources.

For more information, please visit our website at
www.egmont.co.uk/ethical